. . . Love, Emma
XXX

Heartlines

Books by Pam Lyons

A Boy Called Simon
He Was Bad
It Could Never Be
Latchkey Girl
Danny's Girl
Odd Girl Out
Ms Perfect

Books by Anita Eires

Tug of Love
Summer Awakening
Spanish Exchange
Star Dreamer
Californian Summer
If Only...
Teacher's Pet
First Job

Books by Mary Hooper

Love Emma XXX
Follow That Dream
My Cousin Angie
Happy Ever After

Books by Barbara Jacobs

Two Times Two

Books by Jane Pitt

Loretta Rose
Autumn Always Comes
Stony Limits
Rainbow For Sale

Books by Ann de Gale

Island Encounter
Hands Off!

Books by Anthea Cohen

Dangerous Love

Books by David S Williams

Give Me Back My Pride
Forgive and Forget

Books by Gillian Oxley

Change of Heart

Books by Ann Ruffell

Friends For Keeps
Secret Passion

Books by Lorna Read

Images

Mary Hooper

...Love, Emma

XXX

illustrated by Garry Cobb

A Pan Original

First published 1982 by Pan Books Ltd
Cavaye Place, London SW10 9PG
9 8 7 6 5 4 3

ISBN 0 330 26587 3
Printed and bound in Great Britain by
Hunt Barnard Printing Ltd, Aylesbury, Bucks.

Chapter one

Nurses' Home,
Southpark General Hosp.,
London
13th January

Dear Mum and Dad,
Just a few lines to let you know that I arrived safely.

I've been assigned a room in the Home, which is a squat building just behind the main hospital, and I've now unpacked everything on to the three wire coathangers provided (must go on a hunt directly for some more).

We had coffee as soon as we got here – fifteen student nurses eyeing each other up and down and trying to decide who we liked and who we were going to steer clear of. That's what I was doing, anyway.

There were a few girls I took to straight away but I'm no good at first impressions so I'm going to try and keep an open mind about everyone for the time being. We all had to stand up and say our names: 'Emma Rogers,' I said, and it came out all strange and squeaky. Doesn't your name sound funny when you have to say it aloud? I can't remember any of their names; at least, I can remember the names but not the faces that they belong to. I suppose we are all around eighteen, although there is one 'mum-like' figure of about forty-five. I bet she feels a bit out of it.

We were given the clothes which will be our uniform for the next six weeks while we do our preliminary training. Prison wardress on a day out is how they are best described, being slate grey and all approximately the same size and length. Being small, mine is flapping around my ankles somewhere but there is a fairly tall Australian girl whose dress looks more like a skating skirt. At least we don't have to appear on the wards in these; our proper uniforms will be assigned to us before then.

The rooms aren't bad; there is a bed, wardrobe, chest of drawers and sink unit all fitted along one wall, also a drop-down flap with spaces for books, writing paper and all that, where we can sit and study. Along the corridor is a loo and bathroom and down the corridor the other way is a kitchen. There are four other girls sharing the bathroom and loo; I can imagine it gets a bit crowded at peak times. Oh yes, there is also an electric kettle in the room and a few teacups and stuff. Must remember to get some coffee and teabags.

Does my little bedroom look empty and forlorn? I hope you don't keep going in there and sighing heavily, Mum. I will *write as often as I can and come home when I get the chance; promise.*

I'm going off to the canteen now, and then this afternoon is our first proper tutorial. I hope we all start chatting and don't just sit round staring at each other in fright like we did this morning.

Write soon and tell me all the news. If you see any of my friends be sure to tell them I'm enjoying it here (especially those who were highly sarcastic about my being a nurse, like Julie).

Don't forget to take Duncan for walks, or he'll get fat.

Love, Emma xxx

Nurses' Home,
Southpark General Hospital,
London
16th January

Dear Avril,

Hello! Student Nurse Rogers reporting. Yes, it's me, all installed at the hospital and with three whole days' training under my (non-existent) belt.

Haven't exactly saved any lives yet – haven't exactly seen any patients! Have made some perfectly lovely beds, though, and given a succession of blanket baths to a colony of plastic dummy ladies.

Seriously, I'm really enjoying it so far. We (fifteen of us new ones) spend half our time doing practical stuff in pretend wards and the other half listening to lectures and taking notes. It's all very interesting but there's gallons *to learn. My brain is reeling now – I don't know where I'm going to pack in three years' supply of knowledge, really I don't.*

How's the shop? Turned anyone's hair green lately? I'm glad you cut my hair just before I came away, at least you can see there's meant to be a style lurking somewhere beneath the fetching muslin caps we have to wear (just like those worn by the ladies in the delicatessen).

The girls I'm training with are mostly nice. I've made friends with an Australian girl called Beverley who's a real scream and there's a quieter girl called Nicola whom I also like a lot. Then *there's an old bag by the name of Imogen whose dad is a doctor, thus making her (she thinks) infinitely better than us. She and Beverley hated each other on sight and it's made for some interesting confrontations since. There aren't any male student nurses on this intake. All right, all right, I'll get on to the exciting social life and the legions of handsome young doctors next.*

Er . . . there doesn't seem to be any. Social life or *doctors. Well, I did see two white-coated figures disappearing round a corner yesterday but they could have been porters – or figments of my imagination. They are certainly not waiting around, stethoscope in pocket, red rose between teeth, to sweep me into their arms at the hospital dance. Anyway, if one should glance at me now I think he'd jolly quickly glance away; in my revolting uniform and muslin hairnet I'm hardly an object of desire.*

Mind you, when I get on the wards in my black fishnet tights . . .

Seriously, there is *a medical school here, but it's nowhere near the nurses' block. It won't be until we are actually working on the wards that we come into contact with any student doctors. My off-duty life at the moment seems to consist of writing letters, reading text books and falling asleep on my (usually unmade) bed. I feel so tired all the time.*

Have you seen Martin since I left? I must write to him (I've already had two letters from him) but I don't really know what to say. His first letter was a real sloppy one asking me to promise all sorts of impossible things, and then after that came a postcard with Snoopy on it saying 'Miss you'.

I feel tempted to find a card with Snoopy saying 'Don't miss you'. I know it's horrible of me but I can't, haven't got time to, think about Martin now. I've got enough to do without feeling guilty about going away, which is how he's trying to make me feel. If someone asks me out (be positive, Emma, when *someone asks me out) I want to be able to go without feeling awful about Martin. I mean, I haven't promised to remain faithful to him for three years.*

Beverley's just come into my room in a state of great excitement. One of the other girls (Sally) went into Imogen's room and noticed that she had absolutely hundreds of wooden (luxurious-type) coathangers, while all the rest of us had a couple of old wire ones each. Apparently she (Imogen) got here early on Monday, before we got into our

3// .... I think t
go out with
of my train
we may s
LECTUR
Re-readi
of the t
any of
sume
The
Theres
ly)
ke one
vril or
so I pre-
cially.
Garry Cobb

rooms, and 'borrowed' everyone's best hangers. She said to Sally that as she had such good clothes she felt she should have the best hangers to put them on. Beverley has just gone off to claim hers back!

See what excitement we have here? I just knew *it would be like this: life-and-death drama played out under our very noses.*

Oh well, I'd better finish now. Write soon and let me know all that's going on, especially any bits of gossip, no matter how trivial. Talking of trivial bits, have you seen Julie at all? She really annoyed me that last night at your house – all that stuff about a nurse's life being too awful for words and not knowing how I could touch *dirty people. I can't* stand *her. (Don't go and write back saying she's your new best friend now, will you?)*

Love, Emma xxx

Nurses' Home
Southpark General,
London
24th January

Dear Martin,

Thanks for your letters, I don't know how you find the time to write such nice long ones. I suspect you're doing them at work, there were some distinctly greasy fingermarks on that last one!

How is *your dad's garage? You said recently that he might be opening another one; is this still on the cards?*

Of course I've been missing you, but when you ask me if it's as much as you've been missing me I don't know what to say. Life here is so completely different, there's so much to learn and so many new people around, that I don't have time to sit around and mope. I really want to succeed here so I'm not letting myself miss anything *at home too much, because I think that it would hold me back.*

I hope you don't feel I'm being too hard. I don't want to be, but I just don't want you to wait around for three years for me. To be honest, I don't want to wait around for three years myself. I think that we both ought to be free to go out with other people and, who knows, at the end of my training (when I hope to come back and get a job nursing locally) we may still find we've got a lot going for us.

Lecture over! Re-reading that bit above, I realize I sound just like one of the tutors, but I just want to be honest with you.

Well, how is the old place? Have you seen Avril or any of the others? I've heard from Mum (and you) but no one else yet, so I presume life hasn't actually come to a standstill without me.

The girls here are nice, one or two of them especially. There's an Australian girl called Beverley and another one (girl, not Australian) called Nicola who is absolutely stuck on astrology. She can cast her own charts and (she says) is entirely guided by the stars. She swears that if she does a forecast and finds out that it's going to be a bad day she will stay in bed. Can't wait for it to happen and to see the tutor's reaction.

She told me that she sometimes gets 'psychic feelings' about people and I must have looked at her a bit oddly (half expecting her to change me into a frog) because she laughed and said not very often and, not to worry, she didn't intend to go into any trances or anything.

I maybe shouldn't tell you this but she says we are suited, me being Leo and you Aries. She says you are headstrong and determined and there aren't many other zodiac signs who could cope as well as a Leo. I won't tell you what she says about Leos, I'm too modest. Oh – she did say that Leos were bossy, but you know that already.

Tomorrow we are learning how to give injections and the various areas in which they can be done. We've got a dummy with a foam rubber arm to practise on. Just think, it will soon be a real *arm.*

I'll write again as soon as I can.

Lots of love, Emma xxx

Diary

31st January
Nearly three weeks gone and I haven't written down a single thing. I really wanted this to be an accurate, day-by-day account of my training, but maybe it will be month-by-month instead, or just anytime that I've got time.

I miss everyone at home quite a lot – I even miss Martin, though I don't intend to go on about that to him in case he reads more into it than he should. I wonder how I'll feel about him when I go home for my week's break? Maybe I'll find that I've missed him more than I thought – or then again, maybe he will be all small-town and boring and I won't even want him near me.

It was getting a bit like that – with the nearness, anyway – before I left. All he ever wanted to do was get in dark corners with me, and all I wanted to do was find excuses not to. I suppose that really does mean that we haven't got anything going for us. Or I haven't got anything going for him. I know it can't be much good if I have to brace myself to be kissed by him.

Maybe something will happen – I'll meet someone here – and my relationship with Martin will quietly fade into nothing. I must say that the thought of a handsome white-coated medical student is appealing, although knowing that there was a medical school here had absolutely nothing to do with my choice of hospital. Of course not.

I'm gradually getting to know my way around the complex. Apart from the hospital itself, all the administration buildings (canteen, offices, nursing school, lecture halls) are very modern two-storey buildings, set in bits of scrubby earth they have the cheek to call 'gardens'. 'Get orf the bloody garden!' a charming gardener-type person yelled at me yesterday when I was late for a lecture and dared to cross one.

My various trips round the grounds (usually to library or canteen) always seem to take me the longest way round, past the medical school. At first I used to re-do my make-up and put on an earnest, dedicated expression as I hurried by, thinking that hordes of young doctors would be glancing up from their studies and admiring me. But after a week, when I dared lift my eyes and look through the window, I could see that the only lecture room which overlooked the path was completely empty, and it has been ever since. I still go round that way though – ever hopeful.

I'm gradually getting to know the girls better. It usually takes ages to make friends properly but we've all been thrown together so much that already it seems that I've known Beverley and Nicola for years.

Bev was really funny today. We were learning how to bed bath and though we've done it on the 'dummies', tutor said we must practise on each other and we could watch Beverley and Imogen first.

Imogen put on a hospital nightie and climbed into the bed, and Bev set to. Imogen immediately starting moaning and groaning, saying that Bev's hands were too cold, her nails too long and that she was pummelling her.

'There's nothing here worth pummelling,' I heard Bev mutter (Imogen is frightfully thin and elegant) and then Imogen said something about Bev being like a carthorse.

'Shall I scrub the patient's fingernails?' said Bev to tutor, and on receiving the go-ahead she started scrubbing away busily, flicking soap everywhere and practically removing the flesh from Imogen's fingers.

I decided that she was getting her own back for the pinching of the coathangers!

'Not too enthusiastic, dear,' tutor said mildly, and Nicola and I giggled to ourselves.

Bev finished what is loosely termed 'above the waist' and Imogen clutched at her knickers; 'I'm not removing another thing!' she said.

'That's all right,' tutor said, then to Beverley: 'The patient may be left with a bowl of water to wash her own private parts.'

A screen was placed round Imogen and she was left sitting on a rubber sheet, but whether she carried on with the bath we never found out.

We then divided into pairs and blanket-bathed each other. Pretty awkward and uncomfortable it is, too, all those cold trickles of water running where they shouldn't.

'Er . . . what about men?' Bev ventured.

'What about them?' tutor said dryly.

'Their . . . er "private parts",' Bev said, 'we haven't got to do those as well, have we?'

'Not unless the patient is paralysed,' tutor said, 'and be on your guard! A lot of men seem to get temporarily paralysed when there's a brand new nurse on the ward.'

So now we know. Tomorrow – enemas. Don't tell me we've got to practise *those* on each other!

2nd February

Bev has met a medical student – the lucky devil. She went swimming and did some spectacular (her description) dives into the pool, upon which a tall, dark-haired guy approached her and asked her where she learned to dive.

'Melbourne Central,' she said, thus leading the way for a cosy discussion on Swimming-Pools-They-Had-Known.

Nothing like that ever happens to me. When I go swimming I spend half the time daring myself to get in the water and the other half trying to keep my face dry because I've forgotten to put waterproof mascara on.

Anyway, this medic's name is Jeremy and he's in his second year and terribly nice and, no, she didn't find out if he had any friends.

'Are you seeing him again?' I asked.

'Oh, he wanted to know if I swam often and I said yes and that I'd probably see him around,' she said casually.

I do like her attitude. I wish I had it.

I wonder if there's someone here for me? If there is, he can step forward whenever he likes.

Chapter two

Southpark General
10th February

Dear Mum and Dad,
Thanks for your letters and, yes, I am still enjoying it here and am not too homesick. The weekends are the worst, really, as a lot of the girls go home then. It's my own fault, of course, for choosing a hospital 250 miles away from you, but at the time I didn't think much about weekends. One girl actually has a car *sent for her every Friday night (and do we hate her for it!). She comes from a rich family, her dad's a doctor, and I wondered at first why she was slumming it with us in our hospital instead of being at some big posh place, like Guy's. Someone told me today, though, that you have to have 'A' levels to do your training there, so she's obviously only got five 'O's, like the rest of us.*

My six weeks' initial training are almost up now and I'm sitting in the nurses' rest room writing this and waiting for the Allocations Officer to come round and give us our ward allocations. It's all been worked out very scientifically; we're split into groups of three or four (different groups each time) and our movements are mapped out completely for the next three years: ward, school, holiday, test, ward, etc. Once the AO has spoken there is no going back! I'm just dying to get on the wards with real patients. It's been interesting in school, but not like proper nursing.

There is a scuffling in the corner of the room; the AO has come in with our allocations and there's a very un-nurselike flurry towards her. Must go!

Later

Have spent an hour discussing, moaning, comparing and shrieking over our allocations. I'm going to Adelaide, which is a men's surgical ward, and the terrifically posh Imogen is going with me. Beverley and Nicola are on a medical ward and I won't see much of them until we change over back to school in six weeks' time. I'm really excited

about going on the ward, but also am beginning to feel apprehensive. There seems to be about a million things I can do wrong.

We get our uniforms tomorrow. I'll be pleased to get out of this get-up, I can tell you.

I'll write soon and tell you how I get on.

Love, Emma xxx

Southpark General
19th February

Dear Avril,

I'm a real nurse on a real ward! That is, I've got my uniform and am now officially assigned to a men's surgical ward.

The uniform looks fantastic; it's obvious that no one will be able to resist me in it. I look all super-efficient and terribly glamorous (not like me at all). The cap is a bit of a disaster – like a lopsided halo, but you should see the legs encased in black tights! I had set my heart on black stockings with a seam up the back, all 1940-ish, but when I got to the shop I realized I'd have to have a suspender belt, too. Couldn't be bothered with all that so it's just textured black tights. I had to buy them myself, by the way – what a cheek, they aren't classed as part of the uniform.

As soon as I'd been told what my first ward was going to be I dressed up in my uniform and went to have a look at it. It's miles away from the nurses' home, in the oldest block, and a proper Florence

Nightingale old-fashioned ward – rows and rows of beds with a desk for Sister up one end and a sluice room and kitchen at the other.

I wasn't intending to go in, just to have a nose around, but as I was peering through the door a doctor (surgeon?) walked up, followed by two medical students.

'Going in, nurse?' he said to me (nurse*!*).

'Er . . . no, just looking,' I said.

'No extra charge to go in!' he said cheerfully, propelling me through the doors. He was a great big man, almost as wide as he was tall.

So there I was stuck in the middle of the ward, scarlet with embarrassment with all the patients looking at me curiously and the doc and his two hangers-on grinning like mad.

A Sister approached and the three medics disappeared to a patient's bedside.

'Yes?' she said to me.

'I . . . er . . . ' I said. 'I start here tomorrow and thought I'd come and introduce myself.'

'Humph,' she said.

'I'm Nurse Rogers,' I said bravely.

'Bully for you.'

I swallowed. 'See you tomorrow,' I said, backing out of the door.

Once out, I ran down the corridor, remembering quite clearly that a nurse is not supposed to run (apart from haemorrhages and something else that I've forgotten) and not caring. I felt such a fool*!* *I could cheerfully have stuffed that interfering doctor's stethoscope right down his throat.*

After that little incident, I was dreading starting the next day, but it was all right because Sister seemed to have forgotten all about it. Her name is Sister Brunel (yes, she is *built like an ocean liner) and there are three staff nurses on the ward as well as me, Imogen and Sally.*

We have each been assigned a handful of patients and have to carry out life-or-death duties for them: filling their water jugs, tidying their lockers, folding their top sheets smoothly and supplying them with unlimited bedpans! Although that doesn't seem much, you *ought to try doing things under the gaze of Sister Brunel. She steams up and down the ward all the time, her eyes swivelling around like radar equipment, not missing a thing..*

There's one dear old boy in there who slipped me some chocolates today. Most of the patients seem to be getting on a bit, though I notice that Imogen has managed to get herself assigned to the only man under twenty-five in the whole place. Wonder how she managed that?

Thanks for your letter, by the way, and all your news – especially the bit about Julie making a play for Martin. He hasn't even mentioned her to me, though that doesn't mean much. Unless she actually strips off and lays naked in front of him he probably won't realize that she fancies him.

I've thought about how I feel and I don't honestly know if I want to kiss her or kill her. In one way it would be a relief to have Martin off my mind, but on the other hand I wanted to be the one to decide that it was all finished, not him. Yes, I'm as selfish as ever.

Write soon and let me know the latest.

Love, Emma xxx

Southpark General
27th February

Dear Martin,

Sorry I'm taking so long to reply to your letters but I'm on a ward now and really, really busy. The ward is a men's surgical – average age of men, eighty-five. Perhaps that's exaggerating a bit but old, anyhow.

You asked me why my last letter wasn't more personal. I know you mean why wasn't it a love letter, and I don't mean to be horrible but I don't think it would be right to send you long, passionate letters. They wouldn't do either of us any good and would only make the parting seem harder, I think. I also don't want to get caught up in a lot of 'Do you remember the day when . . . ' etc. I'm sure if we both start wallowing in memories we'll only get gloomy and then my work will suffer and you'll be fixing up cars and forgetting to put the wheels on properly or something. You know what I mean.

And please don't think any more about coming to London for the weekend, at least not yet. I'm only just getting myself organized, and though I'd love to see you it would only unsettle me at the moment. Besides, it would cost you a fortune to stay in a hotel round here. Wait until I get my two weeks' leave in the middle of the year and then I'll come home and we can see each other properly. Please.

A clinical teacher – that is, a tutor who comes onto the wards with student nurses – came in today to show us how to prepare someone for surgery. The old boy was actually one of Imogen's assigned patients so she was absolutely full of herself and wouldn't let me or Sally do a thing. She even stepped on my foot when I bent forward to take his thermometer out! 'I'll *do that,' she said smugly, 'there'll be less risk of cross-infection.' Just because we've had half an hour's lecture on cross-infection she thinks she's a world authority on it.*

Anyway, we had to take his temperature, pulse, blood pressure, all the normal stuff, shave him (not *his face, I don't mean) and give him an injection. These duties were supposed to be shared but Imogen got in first every time, the old hag. Once she actually said to Mr Patel, the tutor, 'Oh, my father does it* this *way,' and Sally and I rolled our eyes at each other and waited for an explosion but he didn't say a thing.*

The patient went off to the operating theatre and a couple of hours later Imogen was to be seen standing by his bedside, a long-suffering look on her face and a hand on his brow in approved nurselike manner. Anyone would have thought she'd done the operation herself, single-handed. All I hope is that she clashes head on with Sister Brunel and then she'll get her comeuppance.

Sister Brunel is one step off being matron – or

Nursing Officer as they are called now. She's like a nursing machine, cruises through the ward straightening pillows with one hand, administering enemas and writing up charts with the other. She shouts commands over her shoulder as she goes, but I never seem to get the whole sentence. I hear: 'Mutter . . . mutter . . . specimens, nurse!' or 'Mumble . . . mumble . . . temperature charts!' and then I have to trot after her and ask, ever so politely, if she'll repeat what she said. There's a lovely Indian girl, Staff Nurse Rhena, who rescues me when I get too confused.

Will write again soon,

Lots of love, Emma xxx

Diary

9th March

Ooh, I feel so *stupid*. Who should come into the ward today but the big-wig doctor who made me feel such a fool the other day *and* the two grinning students.

'Oh, nurse,' he said, coming up behind me, 'where's the new RTA?'

'RTA?' I said, searching my mind frantically for what this could be.

'Yes, nurse,' he said impatiently, looking at me as if I was stupid, then he said: 'Oh, it's you – the one who was peering in here last week.' He sounded as if this confirmed I *was* stupid. 'Now, where's the RTA?' he said again.

I made a wild guess because I had no intention at all of confessing that I didn't know what he was talking about. 'I think it's in the equipment room,' I said, and prayed very hard that I'd said the right thing.

God obviously wasn't listening, though, because the three of them burst into hysterics of laughter. As I stood there hoping for the ground to open up Sister sailed into view: 'I know who you've come to see,' she said, then: 'Mutter . . . mutter . . . sluice room,' to me over her shoulder as she led them away.

'RTA is a road traffic accident,' one of the students whispered as they passed me, but I was too humiliated to thank him. I made myself busy in the sluice room until they left, hoping I was doing what Sister wanted me to do. I still feel really stupid.

I wonder how long it's going to take me to get over my embarrassment at being in a ward full of *men*. I'm sure it would have been a lot easier to have started with women. Some of our patients have broken legs and are up on traction, so as well as wanting bottles and bedpans they are also supposed to have their bottoms washed every two hours to prevent bedsores. Some aren't bothered and you can go all day and discover that no one's taken a bowl to old Mr So-and-so, but others – the slightly younger ones – want bowls every two hours. But I've got wise to the bowl business now and since I've started asking a male auxiliary to take it in for me the requests seem to have got fewer.

Caught up with Beverley in the canteen today. She's on a female medical ward and looked at me quite enviously when I told her about the men in traction and the bowls of water.

'The women are so miserable,' she said, 'nothing but moans and complaints all day. Apparently I'm nothing like as good as the last student nurse on the ward, *she* was much more gentle and *she* made them cups of tea after lunch and *she* arranged flowers so beautifully. Makes me sick.'

'Tell me about Jeremy, then. Are you still seeing him?'

'Yes,' she said. 'He's all right – fine.'

'You are lucky. I bet no one else in our student intake is going out with a medic already.'

'Some of us have it, some of us haven't,' she said in a Mae Westish sort of voice.

'You sound just like Imogen,' I said, and pushed her.

'Why don't you come out with us one evening,' she said suddenly. 'I could ask him to bring a friend.'

'Really?'

'Really. We could go down to the social club

or something; they have a group in there two evenings a week.'

So she's seeing him tomorrow to arrange something; I wonder what he'll be like? I haven't had a blind date since I was fourteen – and after that one I swore I'd never have another – but I feel desperately in need of a bit of social life. I'm beginning to get to that gloomy, staring-in-the-mirror-and-wondering-what's-wrong-with-me-stage.

I mean, I'm not *bad* looking, quite acceptable in fact, in a soft pink light, except that I'm a bit plump round the face (compared to someone like Imogen) and my mouth sometimes looks too big for the rest of me. My hair's OK, I suppose, as long as I wash it every other day. Maybe I'll give myself a black rinse or something; I'm fed up with being mousey. I've always fancied being like a heroine in a book I once read with hair as black as a raven's wing. Can't imagine anyone I know coming out with that line.

13th March

I've been off duty a couple of hours, spent ages getting dressed and am now perched on my bed, all made up and raring to go out with Beverley plus two.

Had a pig of a day. Imogen was full of herself, mincing around the ward like she was Sister. Up till now I couldn't understand why Sister and her got on so well, but when I asked Sally about it she said that Imogen told *her* that Sister and Imogen's incredible, best-doctor-in-the-world father trained at the same hospital together and renewed their acquaintance when Imogen came for her preliminary interview. I expect Sister's harbouring a secret passion for him, hard to believe though that is. Anyway, that's why Sister lets her get away with murder.

The most awful thing has happened! As I've been writing this I've been looking out of the window every so often because I was supposed to meet Beverley downstairs in the courtyard. When I looked out a minute ago, though, who should be there with her but those two *horrible* medical students – the ones who keep laughing at me.

I shut my eyes and counted to thirty in the hopes that they were just passing by and had happened to stop for a chat, but when I looked out again one of them had his arm round her and they were all looking at their watches.

Well, I'm *not* going! I can't! What bloody luck – two hundred medical students and I have to get blind-dated with one of those.

It's just on eight o'clock now so I'm going to see if Nicola or Sally will go instead. The guys don't know who's coming so it can't matter to them. If they can't go then I'll have to ask Nicola to take a message to say I've suddenly been taken terribly ill.

It's not *fair*! I'm really fed up.

Southpark General
13th March

Dear Martin,
I know it's only a few days but I haven't heard from you since my last letter and I wonder now if I was too hard on you or said anything which might have upset you.

I've been thinking about you a lot this evening and feeling very lonely. You know I said not *to come for a weekend – well, would you think I was terrible if I changed my mind? I really would like to see you; I don't honestly know if it's because I'm tired or fed up or homesick or what, but I just keep thinking about all the good times we had and wondering if I've done the right thing in coming away.*

Write soon and tell me what you think. If you now don't think it's a good idea to come, I'll try and understand.

Lots of love, Emma xxx

Chapter three

Southpark General
28th March

Dear Mum and Dad,
I'm sorry if the gaps between my letters are getting longer but I am *thinking of you a lot. I'd like to write more often but you know how it is. . .*
I've finished on Adelaide and am now doing my 'block'. That is, the first set of tests with questions connected with what I learnt, or didn't learn, on Men's Surgical. I suppose if you count tidying linen cupboards, emptying bedpans and whipping thermometers out of patients' mouths I know quite a lot. No, I'm only joking, I did learn more than that and things are very gradually beginning to fall into place, though the amount still to learn horrifies me.
A girl called Jane who started with us is talking about dropping out. She says that the work is too hard for her and that they expect too much of us. It is *and they* do, *but I knew it would be like this before I started so it's not so much of a shock.*
Have you seen anything of Martin? I had a letter saying that he was thinking of coming down for the weekend to see me, and then another saying that he would come to you for directions from the

railway station. I hope he warns me exactly when he's arriving because when I get on the next ward my shifts will be different: seven thirty to four thirty or one to nine, four days on, two days off, whether it's the weekend or not. I'm wondering now if I did the right thing in saying he could come; I wrote when I was feeling really miserable and fed up. Still, it'll be nice to see him and he wanted to come.

At the moment I seem to spend most of my weekends sleeping. Apart from the fact that I'm tired all the time I find that if I sleep most of Sunday it cuts down on the number of meals I've got to buy. We can go into the hospital canteen at weekends if we want to, but nearly everyone chooses to cook their own. The kitchen at the end of

the hall is full of smoke and swear-words by three o'clock on a Sunday.

I went for a walk with Beverley around London last weekend. Considering one of the reasons I chose to train down here was to be where the bright lights and action were, I've not seen any. *We walked round the City, St Paul's, Eastcheap and Fleet Street. Once we got away from the touristy bits it was very peaceful and old, like going back in time. Then Beverley insisted on bringing us down to earth; she had to be photographed outside Australia House, looking like a lunatic.*

While doing this block we are taking the occasional trip to the other hospital departments, just to see how they all work together. I'm for Accident and Emergency on Monday morning; hope I don't see anything too gory.

Love, Emma xxx

Southpark General
9th April

Dear Avril,
I've done something really stupid; I could kick myself. A while back Beverley arranged a blind date for me, but when I looked out of my window that night who should be waiting for me but the two awful *medical students I spoke to you about – well, I thought they were awful. I suppose I should have gone and braved it out with them but there*

had been another embarrassing incident in the ward since the one I told you about, and I just couldn't.

So I asked Nicola to go instead of me and, yes, you guessed it, she had a fantastic time and came back saying how fabulous my one was (his name was Luke) and fancy me not wanting to go and he's the most interesting, witty person she's ever met in her life, etc. And *she's been out with him a couple of times since.*

When she asked me why I didn't want to go in the first place I just said that I didn't like the look of him, so now when she keeps talking about him I have to pretend to be all bored and keep saying 'Oh, really?' in a disinterested way, but really I'm absolutely GREEN.

Beverley's 'gone off' me too because she arranged it specially for me, so altogether I'm in the doghouse.

Damn and blast. I know *I should have gone and just laughed it off with them but it's much too late now – and meanwhile Beverley and Nicola are the envy of the whole of our intake. Grr. . .*

As if that wasn't bad enough, I got so miserable I actually wrote to Martin and asked him to come and visit for a weekend. I must be mad. *I regretted the letter immediately my hand was in the post box, but I couldn't get it out! So, he's going to arrive some weekend soon, all hot-foot and eager and thinking I am, too – and in the meantime* I've *gone off* him.

Anyway (I haven't finished yet), two days ago when I was in Accident and Emergency for the morning I met someone. He's very nice, not a doctor, or a blooming medical student, but a young police constable.

We were down there assisting with the filling in of cards and shuffling people around into different queues when I saw him come in with an elderly lady. He looked ghastly – I mean, he was good-looking, but ghastly pale.

'Are you the patient?' I said to him. Well, he looked worse than her.

'No, this lady is,' he said, and he smiled faintly. 'Do I look that bad, then?'

I nodded sympathetically with my best caring-nurse face. 'If you'd both like to sit down,' I said. 'What's the trouble?'

The old dear pointed to what looked like a red striped towel which was covering her arm. 'Cut it with one of them newfangled electric carving knives,' she said. I then noticed a trail of blood coming from the door to us and felt my knees go all wobbly. I plonked her into a wheelchair and wheeled her off to be seen to straight away.

'Thanks,' he said when I came out. 'She walked all the way to the police station with that.'

'You'd better sit down and rest,' I said.

'Hot sweet tea for shock, isn't it?' he said. 'Care to join me?'

'I'm not allowed to,' I said, thinking that it must be the black tights working at last. 'Sorry.'

'That's a shame. Some other time, perhaps,' he said, and off he went.

Nicola, though, who was with me in Accident,

said (when she could stop talking about Luke) that he was outside the hospital today; so maybe, just maybe, he's hanging about looking for me.

I hope so. But maybe it would be better if he delayed his approach until Martin's been and gone. At least I'll be able to talk to Martin with a clear conscience: 'Of course I haven't been out with anyone else, darling.' Worse luck.

11th April

Should have posted this but couldn't find a stamp. However, further news of policeman – he was in Casualty today filling out a police accident form for the old dear he brought in and, as luck would have it, I was there for the afternoon too.

Anyway, we got chatting and he said he had to have my name and rank for this form. 'And phone number,' he added.

'Is that strictly necessary?' I said.

'It is for my little black book,' he said.

So I gave him the number of the nurses' home and now I'm in his LBB. Don't know if I like being in an LBB but I suppose it's better than nothing.

I've made it up with Beverley, too, so that's all right. Over lunch in the canteen she was telling me about Jeremy and Luke and some of the jokes they've got up to whilst being medical students – putting skeletons in people's beds and all the usual sort of stuff. She said that they are really just as unsure of themselves as we are and it's quite a relief to find out that nurses, all highly polished and efficient, sometimes don't know much.

'There was some nurse who told them that they could find a road traffic accident victim in the equipment room!' she said, and roared with laughter.

Stony silence from me, then I took a deep breath. 'OK – joke over. That was me!'

More hysterics.

'Well, did you know what RTA stood for before you were told?'

Hysterics subsided a little. 'I suppose not.'

'See!'

'Oh – it all falls into place – that's why you wouldn't come on the blind date!'

'Exactly.'

'Oh, you fool! You could have made a big joke about it; they would have enjoyed that.'

'I'm sure they would have.'

'No, really. I wish you'd have come. Luke's really great.'

I said that I kept hearing he was. I suppose Bev'll tell them now why I didn't come. Ooh, I hope I don't see him any more.

Love, Emma xxx

PS You didn't mention Julie in your last letter. Is she still after Martin or has she found someone else to vamp?

Southpark General
13th April

Dear Martin,
Thanks for you letters and don't worry about not being able to get here for a few days yet. I quite understand about your not being able to leave the garage.

I'm glad you're looking forward to seeing me so much – yes, of course I'm looking forward to seeing you. It will be lovely to talk about things and people unconnected with the hospital.

Found out today that I passed my last block (exam) OK. We all have, actually, apart from a girl called Mandy who has to do another six weeks on the same ward and then sit it again. (Big *disgrace; we are all looking pretty smug because we've passed.) There is also a girl called Jane who has dropped out completely – gone home without waiting to find out if she passed or not.*

I've just started on Farringdon, which is a women's medical ward, and I'll be here for eight weeks. Hardly know the staff yet but at first glance they don't seem as terrifying as the last lot; there is no one like Sister Brunel, for instance (there couldn't be two *like that). I'm on with Cathy and Imogen – again. I think someone up there must have it in for me, putting her and me together again, though I think Cathy might sort her out a bit. We were sitting around at coffee time and Imogen was talking (yawn) about the way her father gets on with everyone and what a wonderful doctor he is when Cathy suddenly said:*

'Your father sounds a right twit.'

'I beg your pardon?' Imogen said.

'Hearing about him proper gets on my nerves.'

I giggled before I could stop myself and Imogen looked at us both witheringly. 'That's no more than I would expect from the likes of you,' she said. 'You're not fit to hear me speak about him.'

'That's good!' Cathy said. 'Let's not, then.'

Maybe that will shut her up a bit.

What have you been doing with yourself at weekends? Have you seen anything of Julie or any of the others?

See you soon, then. Try and ring to let me know what train you'll be on and I'll get to the station if I can. If all else fails, though, get a taxi to the hospital and the nurses' home is just behind it – you can't miss it.

Lots of love, Emma xxx

Diary

27th April

Had a terrible day – have witnessed my first death. Everyone said to me after that the first one is always the worst and that death won't be such a mysterious and unknown quantity any more but I don't know about that. I still feel pretty shaky.

The woman was very old – eighty-four, I think, but a real old darling with beautiful snow-white hair and a pink and white wrinkled face. She was one of the nicest women on the ward. Always had a kind word and whenever she asked for anything added, 'if it's not too much trouble, nurse', so you didn't mind what you did for her.

She was a heart patient; don't know exactly what she had but I knew it was her heart from the drugs she was taking. This last couple of days she had only been able to speak in a whisper and said she was cold all the time, though she had piles of hot water bottles and blankets.

I was sitting with her this afternoon just doing general observation when I noticed that she'd gone quite blue round the lips and her skin was clammy.

I called Sister and she took one look at her and told me to pull the curtains round. She bent over her and after a moment straightened up.

'The poor old love's gone,' she said.

'Oh God!' I said, and I closed my eyes and was scared to look at her. I knew I was being stupid but I'd never seen a dead body before.

'Nothing to be frightened of,' Sister said kindly. 'She's just as harmless now as she was before. It was a nice, peaceful end for her.'

So I opened my eyes and looked and Sister had laid her down and she just looked as if she was sleeping, but quite vacant and empty somehow.

'I'll get Staff in to do the necessary; you go and have a cup of tea,' she said to me, so I did.

And that was it; my first death. Don't suppose they'll all be as easy and uncomplicated as that, though.

29th April

Just spent the most embarrassing minute of my life. As I was coming out of the ward *who* should I bump into but that Luke guy. Might have known I would sooner or later.

I literally *did* bump into him and I looked up, saw it was him and started to scurry away.

'What's wrong with me, then?' he said.

'What. . . what do you mean?'

'You stood me up the other night and now you can't get away fast enough,' he said, half-joky and half-serious.

'I didn't. It was only a blind date. You didn't know it was me who was supposed to come and not Nicola.'

'Didn't I?' he said teasingly. 'How do you know I didn't ask for you specially?'

I stared at him for a moment and then I mumbled something about going on duty and dashed away. He's never seen me when I haven't been dying of embarrassment; he must think I'm naturally scarlet in the face.

Went straight to Beverley's room (where she was flat out after a day in Adelaide with Sister Brunel). Didn't mention having just seen him, but managed to wriggle the conversation round to dates, and blind dates in particular. There was something I just had to know!

'I mean, you never know who you're going to end up with unless you've asked to meet someone in particular, and then it's not a blind date, is it?' I said casually.

'No,' she said, yawning.

'I mean, they – Jeremy and Luke – didn't know we were friends, did they?'

'I suppose not,' she said, scratching her head so that her cap fell forward over her nose. 'Wait, though. Jeremy did say to bring my pretty dark-haired friend – I thought it was him who'd seen you with me, but perhaps it was Luke.'

'Oh,' I said.

'Why are you so interested, anyway? I thought you couldn't stand him.'

'No, I can't!' I said heatedly. 'I was just talking generally. Anyway, Nicola's going out with him now.'

I can't stop wondering if he did ask for me to go. Feel even more confused about him than ever. Suppose he actually *fancied* me and I passed him up? No, he couldn't have. Silly to think about it now, anyway.

Later

This must be my day. The phone in the hall went just now, as it does continually this time of the evening. I hardly notice it any more because it's never for me – or wasn't up till tonight.

It was Jon, the policeman, asking me if I'd like to go for a meal in the Carvery on Friday. Bev's been there and it's a restaurant where you can eat as much meat as you like – until you're sick, she said. Agreed to go, of course, then rushed up the hall to tell Bev and Nicola.

'Find out his birth sign,' Nicola said.

'Before we've eaten or after? If it's wrong can I still have a meal?'

'After will do. I'll tell you if you're suited,' she said.

'She's only eating with him, not moving in,' Bev said.

1st May (Friday)

Got up late this morning and charged through the hall, snatching up two letters as I ran.

Only had time to open them at coffee break. One was from Avril and other from Martin – saying that he would be arriving tonight and could I meet the train!

I could spit! Immediately zoomed to call box in rest room and spent the entire coffee break trying to locate Jon. I know which station he's at but because he's still training he's often out and about at different places and sometimes doesn't go to it for days. I've left messages in various places and just hope that he gets them.

Of course, I wish now that I'd never asked

Martin in the first place. Suppose Jon doesn't get the message and thinks I've stood him up?

Oh, blast everything.

Chapter four

Southpark General
Monday 4th May

Dear Mum and Dad,
I've had a hectic month! Thanks for the letters and the photographs of Duncan. He looks fatter and scruffier than I remember! Are you sure you're taking him for enough walkies?

I expect you've heard that Martin came up on Friday night. We had a good weekend even though I had to go on duty on Sunday. Martin found he had booked himself into a really seedy hotel where there seemed to be all sorts of strange goings-on, so I think he was quite pleased to be going home early. He booked it through an evening paper so didn't know what he was getting into; there were 'ladies of dubious character' staying there!

We saw a few sights and went round the art galleries on Saturday. I liked the Tate best; there were the most beautiful paintings tucked away in a room downstairs. Pre-Raphaelite, they were called (hope I've spelt it right), and they are absolutely breathtaking. I had to be forcibly removed from the room otherwise I would have stayed there all day.

A really mixed weekend, you might say – arts and tarts, Martin called it.

I'm enjoying my new ward – Farringdon, women's medical. Sister O'Neill, who's in charge, is small and wiry and, maybe because she's so tiny, not nearly as frightening as Sister Brunel. She's sharp as anything, though, has got little beady eyes that can spot a crumpled sheet from 500 yards, but she really doesn't bother us new nurses too much. I suppose we're too lowly for her to even think about; we get most of our orders from the staff nurses.

When Bev was on this ward she said that the women complained a lot, and I've found that to be true. They are much worse than the men, always finding fault and quibbling about things.

There's a Mrs Simpson in particular who seems to think that I've been put on the ward specially to attend to her every fancy. She called me over today to say that the woman in the next bed had a bigger portion of jelly than her, and what did I intend to do about it? Yesterday, when most of the other nurses were up at the other end of the ward with one of the doctors, she called me, saying it was 'awfully urgent'.

'Just one minute,' I said, flying past with swabs for the doctor.

'Nurse! You'll have to come!' she said.

'One moment, Mrs Simpson!' charging by with specimen dish.

'I can't. . . ' her voice died away to a faint whisper.

At last I got to her, thinking that she was dying, and do you know what she said: 'I can't find my apple. Someone's stolen it from my fruit bowl.'

Write soon,

Love, Emma xxx

PS This afternoon one of the patients asked me wistfully when that 'lovely Australian nurse' was coming back – she was so *kind and helpful. That really is a scream because Bev said they were always moaning and wanting to know when the student nurse before* her *was returning!*

Southpark General
Wednesday 13th May

Dear Avril,

Thanks for your last letter, which arrived the same time as one from Martin saying he was arriving that night and would I meet the train!

I was pleased to see him, of course, but would have been even pleasder (all right, so there's no such word) if he hadn't been arriving on the day I had a date with Jon, the policeman. So while I was at the station waving a white hanky from the back of the crowd I should have been wining, dining and playing footsie under the table with Jon.

I left messages at half a dozen police stations but I still don't know if he got them because he hasn't been in touch. Perhaps he just sat there, roast beef slowly congealing in front of him, all night. I hope he doesn't think I just stood him up; he's my only hope of a social life down here.

Anyway, to get back to Martin: when I first saw him I felt this big rush of affection for him and thought, yes, he is *the one for me and how could I ever have doubted it? It was so lovely to see a familiar face.*

As the weekend wore on, though, and the novelty of having him there wore off, it got to be just like it was at home, with him wanting to kiss me all the time and me finding it all a bit tedious.

I can't remember now if I've always felt like this about him kissing me, or whether he didn't do it so much early on so it didn't get to be a rather boring habit, but anyhow he seemed to be doing it on average once every thirty seconds or so. I'd just got interested in the film or had shoved a bit of hamburger in my mouth when his face would loom into view, lips all puckered, and then I'd have to close my eyes hastily, swallow the bit of hamburger or whatever, and prepare for action. I didn't like to appear unfriendly when he'd come 250 miles to see me so I couldn't shove him away or anything. Maybe he was deprived of affection as a child – or maybe I'm a bit frigid.

Dear Auntie Avril,
Is there something wrong with me?

So, all in all, I was fairly pleased that I had to go on duty on Sunday.

He was staying in a right scream of a place in the 'red light district' I think they call it. When I met him at the station we caught a taxi to take us to his 'hotel' (and no wonder the driver looked at me a bit funny) which was a four or five-storey house with Ethelbrook Hotel in green neon lights over the door.

There were two floosies (as my Mum would say) sitting on the reception desk; one had a dressing gown on and the other had a boob tube, split skirt and not much else.

They brightened up a bit when Martin walked in, but then I trotted in after him and their faces fell. They gave him a key to a room on the top floor (no lift) which was awful. It smelt of fried onions and was small, dark and grim. Martin said there were doors banging and people rushing around all night and he didn't fancy getting in between the sheets so he slept on top of the bed with his clothes on. If he ever had thoughts of coming to London to seduce me they must have vanished as soon as he saw the room – definitely not a seduction parlour!

So he went back and nothing's really changed. We haven't decided anything about our relationship; just said we'd carry on writing and I'd see him when I come home on holiday in July.

He talked about you and the others but didn't mention Julie once, by the way. Significant?

I'm on a new ward now, did I tell you? I actually gave an injection on my own, in a real arm, today. The patient was this old fusspot of a woman who shrieks the place down if you so much as remove a sticking plaster from her, so I was dreading it. But Cathy came in with me and actually made her laugh by asking her whether she

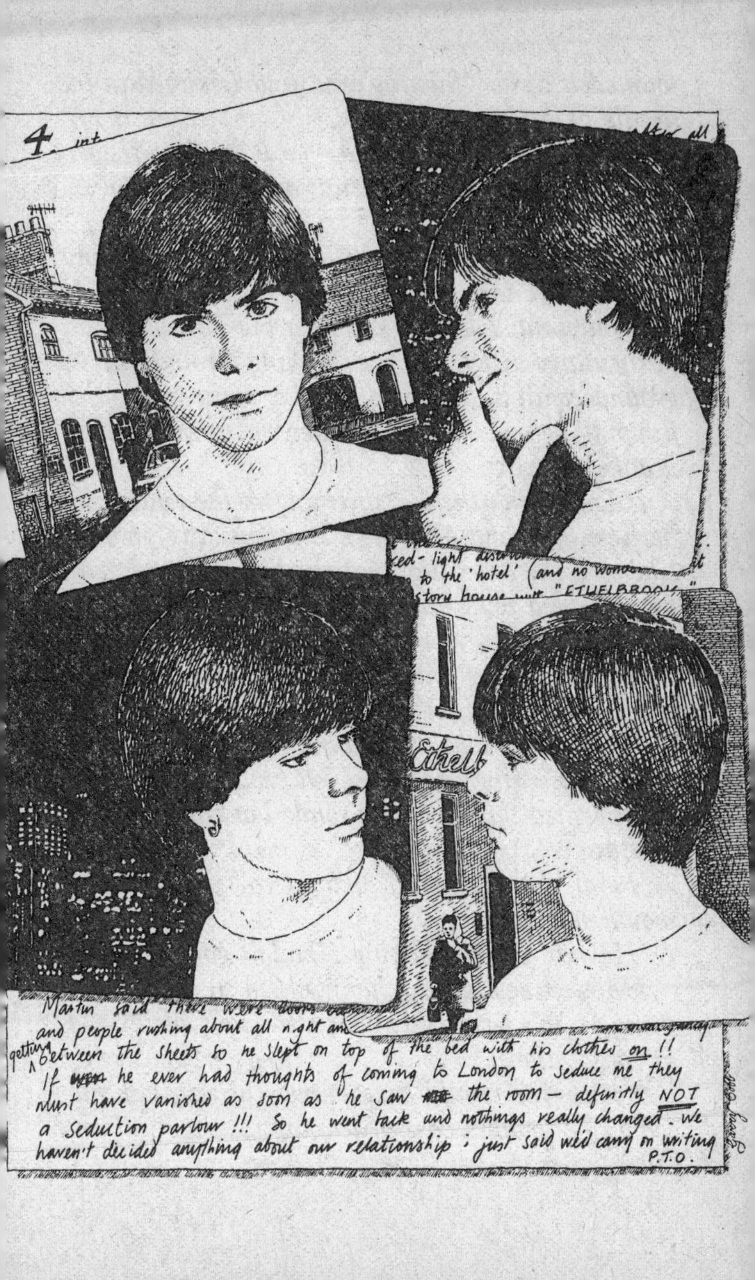
4.
to the 'hotel' (and no
Martin said there were
and people rushing about all night an
getting between the sheets so he slept on top of the bed with his clothes on !!
If he ever had thoughts of coming to London to seduce me they
must have vanished as soon as he saw the room – definitly NOT
a seduction parlour !!! So he went back and nothings really changed. We
haven't decided anything about our relationship : just said we'd carry on writing
P.T.O.

wanted it in her 'bum or arm' and I jabbed in the needle before she noticed it.

I think she was mad afterwards because she'd been hoping to have hysterics, and get me into trouble.

Bev and Nicola are still going out with Jeremy and Luke. I saw him (Luke) at a distance yesterday and I hate to admit it but he looked particularly dishy. He was rushing through the grounds with a distracted air, his white coat flapping behind him. Reminded me of the White Rabbit in Alice.

I don't think there is anything in the relationship between him and Nicola (I keep casually probing). She said the other day that she didn't intend getting too involved with him because he is Sagittarius and she is Taurus.

'What's wrong with that?' I said, all innocent of the astrological significance.

She made a whistling sound through her lips. 'Fire and earth; earth puts out fire,' she said.

I puzzled this out for a while but couldn't seem to draw any conclusions.

'Now, you're fire too, being Leo,' she said. 'You would suit him.'

'Ha ha,' I said, hoping I hadn't gone red.

He is *nice; I wish I hadn't been so hasty. Still, I expect he's terrifically conceited (says she by way of consolation).*

I wish Jon would contact me. I'd ring him but it would be another case of leaving messages all over the place again. Perhaps my name has been deleted from the LBB.

Did I tell you about this fabulous shop just near the hospital? It's called Lily and sells all sorts of Victorian and old clothes, and quite cheap. I. bought a silk blouse which has about a million little hand-done tucks all down it, and Bev bought a gen-u-ine 1920s flapper dress with (rather fraying) fringes all over it. Isn't it great to have your own money to spend? I remember you telling me that when you started at the hairdresser's. Mind you, our pay is a pittance and when we've paid our board there's hardly anything left, but still. . .

Nearly forgot, I tried to dye my hair black. I did it on the Friday I had the date with Jon (which turned out to be a date with Martin) and managed to turn everything within six yards of the sink black – the tiles, flannels, toothbrush, my scalp and fingernails. The off-white mat which goes round the sink now looks like a dead dalmatian. Everything went black except my hair; it washed out of that beautifully leaving it dark mouse as usual. Where did I go wrong?

Write soon,

Love, Emma xxx

Southpark General
22nd May

Dear Martin,
Glad to hear you got home safely. It was a lovely weekend; thanks for coming. I'm sorry I had to go on duty on Sunday, but you know how it is.

Pity about your hotel! If you come up again I'll scout around first and view the places before you book.

I didn't ask you much about your new garage; felt guilty about that afterwards. Have you actually signed for the new premises? Will you be in charge of the old one once your dad takes over the new?

Life on Farringdon goes on more or less as normal. We had a consultant's round today, which meant everything in the ward had to be polished to within an inch of its life. All the sheets and pillowslips had to be changed and the patients smartened up. If they were at all capable of doing so they had to be sitting up and looking brightly around them, if they were too ill to do that they had to lie flat. No lolling about propped up on elbows or anything slovenly like that. I've found out that Sister O'Neill is one of the old school when it comes to consultants' rounds.

I've told you about Imogen before; well, she managed to ingratiate herself with Mr Thomas, the number two man in the hospital, by passing him a patient's chart before he'd even asked for it. All he said was: 'Can I see this. . . ' and she'd put it in his hand.

'Thank you, *nurse,' he said, looking at the*

simpering Imogen, 'good training, eh what?' (This to the rest of his followers.)

'My father. . . ' Imogen said delicately, with fifteen pairs of eyes on her. And then followed one of the conversations we've come to know and love: 'He trained at St Thomas's in the early fifties. . . ' etc. The awful thing is all the doctors and consultants seem actually interested in hearing about him; they don't seem to be just being polite.

Told Bev about it at lunchtime and she said darkly that we'd have to 'do something'. Honestly, Imogen is full of herself and seemingly un-put-downable. She told us for the twentieth time today how this time last year she went to one of the Queen's garden parties with Mummy and Daddy 'and the Queen herself remarked on my outfit'. Believe that if you like.

We are heavily into astrology here at the moment. At least, Nicola is telling us things about our characters according to our birth signs and we are saying 'yes' to the bits that we like and 'certainly not' to the bits that we don't.

Bev and I got half a dozen morning papers together in the canteen at lunchtime just to try and prove to her that it's a lot of rubbish. (One of the perks of the job – pinching the patients' newspapers.) We cut them up and got them all sorted out and they were ridiculous. One said Leo would have a 'wonderful day, rich in opportunities' and another said 'a day in which you'd be wise to stay in bed' and the rest came somewhere in between. Nicola wouldn't have it, though. She said she doesn't believe daily horoscopes anyway, but goes by her own birth chart (which she cast herself) and judges good and bad days by the planets surrounding her. So there.

Oh yes, she also said that Taurus is a sign of healing and more doctors and nurses are born under it than any other sign. Suppose it would be interesting to take a survey in the hospital but I'm not going to do it. I seem to do enough scatty things already.

Will write again soon,

Lots of love, Emma xxx

Diary

29th May

Sat down a week ago to write this, hoping to occupy a dead night, and as I did so the phone outside rang and it was Jon.

The same trick hasn't worked tonight though, so I'll carry on and fill up a few pages with what has been happening.

When Jon phoned I was so pleased to hear from him – someone – *anyone* that I forgot to be all cool, even when he shattered me by saying how sorry he was that he hadn't been able to make our date and he hoped I'd got his message!

'*You* couldn't make it?' I said. '*I* couldn't make it either.'

'Really? That was lucky.'

But I didn't know if he believed me or not, it must have sounded suspiciously as if I was trying to save my own face.

He said he'd had to go and attend a big parade up North to give him some insight into crowd control, and then straight after that he went on a course. He didn't receive *any* of the messages I left round the stations for him, and I certainly didn't receive his.

'I rang the nurses' home number loads of times and it was engaged,' he said, 'and then I got some posh-sounding girl who was terribly vague about whether she knew you or not. I explained what you looked like' (wonder what he said?) 'and told her your first name and she said she "rally couldn't say" if she knew you. I had to leave then so I asked her to do her best and try and find you.'

Realized immediately he was talking about Imogen and that I would like to steam her in the sterilizing unit, but I'll write a bit more about that later.

Jon then asked to see me the next night and I went, of course, and was terribly excited about going, but I can't help feeling a tiny bit disappointed now. He was very nice and all that, but he talked about himself non-stop. I know all those How-to Handle-Your-First-Date-With-Him articles say you're supposed to encourage them to speak about themselves but he didn't need any encouragement and I'd have liked to get the occasional remark in sideways.

He *was* entertaining, though, and at least we weren't sitting around frantically trying to fill the silences, but I don't believe he's going to be the love of my life – which is a shame, because there don't appear to be any other candidates.

Perhaps he was just nervous. I suppose I'd better reserve judgement on him at least until we've had another date – in two days' time. He didn't ask to see me the next day or anything – not that I really wanted to see him, but it would have been nice if he hadn't been able to live without me. Was a bit nervous that he would leap on me after driving me home, but he didn't, so that's one thing in his favour.

He's all right. Perhaps I'm just expecting too much. Life's not like it is in magazine stories, but I never stop hoping that it will be.

Funny, I don't feel the slightest bit guilty about going out with him behind Martin's back, but I'm sure I would if I thought that there was going to be anything significant between me and Jon.

Back to Imogen (Bev calls her 'Immo' which annoys her no end); I tackled her the same day about Jon's call and she said she couldn't remember it and that anyway, she couldn't be expected to run round delivering messages like a servant!

I was speechless. I couldn't think of anything

really cutting to say, so I just walked away. She's only got to be there for me to feel inferior to her, anyway. She's so elegant and poised that I naturally feel small and scruffy in comparison.

Anyway, she put Bev down the next day over something or other so we thought of A PLAN. Beverley asked Jeremy to get us an *eye*. Not a real one, a glass one – but it looked really lifelike.

We placed this in Imogen's make-up bag one evening after supper. It was really gratifying; she went off to reapply her Chanel No. 5 or whatever and we heard a bloodcurdling scream and she rushed out of the loo as if someone was chasing her with a hypodermic. Bev immediately dashed in and retrieved the eye, and then we all sat round innocently while she came back with one of the tutors and they searched for it.

I'd like to say that she'd been a changed person ever since, but she hasn't. Only today she had a tantrum because one of her monogrammed towels had been lost in the hospital laundry. Bev says she can't decide what to plant on her next – a piece of sheep's intestine from a biology lesson or an artificial leg.

1st June

Getting ready to go out with Jon but am finding it difficult to concentrate on glamorizing myself. Reason: Nicola has just wandered up to say that, by the way, she's not going out with Luke any more.

Thumpetty-thump. . . I heard my heart go and then I said all casually, 'Oh, why's that?'

She shrugged. 'Oh, you know. He's nice and all that but it was never any big deal. I went really just to make up numbers.'

'What about Jeremy and Bev, though?'

'Oh, they're all right. I wouldn't be surprised if they ended up quite serious about each other.'

'But not you and er. . . Luke.' I thought that was a nice touch, as if I couldn't quite remember his name.

'I've got too much hospital work to do to bother about boyfriends,' she said. 'But you, though. . . I've got a funny feeling about you and Luke.'

'But I've never. . . I don't even know him! I've hardly spoken to him!' I said quickly.

'I don't mean now, silly, I mean in the future,' she said, and her eyes got all far-away, like they do sometimes. 'He's no good for me, anyway – Taurus and Sagittarius!'

'Nearly forgot,' I said. 'Earth and air.'

'Earth and *fire*.' And she wandered out, leaving me still thumpetty-thumping loudly to myself.

Chapter five

Southpark General
Friday 5th June

Dear Mum and Dad,
These are my last few days on Women's Medical and they've been really hectic. Someone said that it was supposed to be the quiet time of the year for hospitals but this ward seems to have a permanent rush on.

Did a late duty yesterday so I went round with Night Sister giving out the sleeping pills. Discovered one patient with a little secret hoard of them! We are supposed to stand with each patient and make quite sure the pills are taken, but apparently this particular old dear had been pushing them into her cheek and then removing them as soon as Sister had passed on to the next bed. She's been in hospital for weeks so she had about fifty of them all stored in a barley sugar bag.

'Ah ha!' Sister said triumphantly, spying the bag in her locker, 'setting up shop were we, Mrs Tyler?'

'We were doing no such thing,' Mrs Tyler said (she's old but she's got all her marbles), 'we were merely avoiding being nagged at by Sister, who insists on a sleeping pill whether we want one or not.'

Sister didn't say anything else, just carried the bag away and dramatically flushed the offending pills down the loo.

I've discovered that Night Sister and Sister O'Neill hate each other. Sister O'Neill leaves lots of pointed notes around for Night Sister: 'Please leave this sluice room as you would wish to find it'; 'Kindly do not attempt to change dressing on Mrs Burton's leg' and 'Please ensure that night staff do not attempt duties of which they are not capable'. When she comes on duty in the morning she darts about looking at things, inspecting the patients behind the ears to see that they've been washed properly and (I'm sure) hoping against hope that Night Sister's neglect will have caused someone to die in the night. She'd like to stay on duty twenty-four hours a day, I think, just to ensure that her ward doesn't fall into anyone else's hands.

Mum, can you remember the exact time I was born – to the minute? Nicola is going to cast a horoscope chart for me.

I finish in Farringdon on the seventh and then start three weeks of study concentrating on aspects of care in Women's Medical with an exam at the end of it – then HOME for two weeks. Impossible to think that the first six months has gone by so quickly.

Don't get a lot of visits planned, I just want to laze about, see a few friends and sleep.

Really looking forward to seeing you all. Feel terribly guilty; have been meaning to write to Gran

for weeks – but perhaps you've been passing these letters onto her anyway to keep her in touch.
Love, Emma xxx

Southpark General
14th June

Dear Avril,
Have been attending lectures on pulmonary diseases and rheumatoid arthritis so it's a real break to write to you. Am sitting outside at the moment; there's a small strip of grass in front of the nurses' home and I'm writing to you and trying to get a little bit of a tan at the same time.

I eventually heard from Jon, and have been out with him twice. The second time was better than the first, I actually managed to speak that time. Not a lot, mind you. . .

He's very nice and good company but a bit too full of himself for my liking. He's never short of a funny story and is very considerate and everything, but I'm just not sure that I'm not one of a whole chain of girls he's busy being considerate to. He's a bit flash; a bit 'nudge, nudge, say-no-moreish'. Know what I mean?

Oh dear, I've made him sound awful. He's not that bad. I should worry, anyway. It's nice to be taken out occasionally, and the fact that he doesn't find me the most desirable female on earth should be a relief really. At least it doesn't complicate things.

Big news of the month: Luke and Nicola have broken up! Have been unable to discover, even by asking Bev, who exactly did the breaking, but anyway they have. I've walked past the medical school loads of times since then (purely for the exercise, of course) but I haven't seen anything of him. I don't want to actually meet him, because he always reduces me to a pink embarrassed lump, but I'd quite like to gaze upon him from afar. Would die rather than admit it to anyone but you but he's got gradually dishier everytime I've seen him. Don't think *it's just the mystique that always surrounds the godlike white-coated figure of a doctor, there are too many of them around here for that – and anyway, the Sisters put them down at every opportunity.*

Doubt if I'll see him before I come home anyway, because at the moment we're back in school for three weeks then after my holiday it's on to the great unknown pastures of the maternity unit.

I was sorry to leave Farringdon, really. In eight weeks you come to know the patients really well, especially the long-term ones, and can get quite attached to them and their funny little ways. I know exactly how many minutes Mrs Patterson likes her eggs boiled, that Mrs Simpson likes her cornflakes without milk and that Mrs Parfitt likes the bedpan warmed before it's put underneath her, and now all this encyclopaedia of information has gone for nothing.

Had a small drama on my last day. One of the younger patients, a rather 'glam' woman called Mrs

Ford who was only in for observation, had a visitor every afternoon who everyone took to be her husband.

A real love match, I used to think as I watched her do herself up every afternoon with false eyelashes, blue glittery eyeshadow and fluffy pink bedjacket (well, she was like that); how nice that she still makes an effort for her husband.

On this particular day he'd arrived as usual and been greeted with kisses, then 'Mr and Mrs Ford' had half-pulled the curtain around the bed and sat cosily talking (?) inside it. I'd just started doing a temperature round with one of the staff nurses when suddenly a man appeared at the end of the ward clutching a brown paper bag that looked as if it contained fruit.

'Excuse me, nurse,' he said to me, 'when will I be allowed to visit my wife?'

'Well, if she's really ill you'd better check with Sister,' I said.

'Oh, she's not ill.'

'Anytime, then. It's open visiting in the afternoons on this ward.'

'Oh?' he said. 'She told me that she couldn't have visitors. This is Farringdon Ward, isn't it?'

'Yes,' I said, confused. Staff was glowering at me to carry on with the temperature round with her. 'What's your wife's name?'

'Ford. Angela Ford.'

Gulp!

'Er. . . I'll just go and see if she's. . . awake,' I said, and I walked swiftly down the ward and into

the curtained love-nest containing the 'Fords' to find them rolling passionately on the bed! It could have been worse, I suppose – he could have been inside the sheets!

I coughed loudly. 'Excuse me,' I said, 'but your husband is here.'

Mrs Ford sat up swiftly and smoothed down her fluffy bedjacket (which had all its fur disarrayed as if it had been fighting) and he *swung his feet on to the floor. At that moment the real Mr Ford, who'd followed me down the ward apparently, bounded in through the curtains and they confronted each other, High Noon style.*

Mrs Ford burst into tears, washing away her false eyelashes in the process, and there then followed a short skirmish during which the curtains round the bed billowed and bundled and were eventually pulled off their runners. Mr Ford's grapes were trampled to the floor. The rest of the ward, their own visitors forgotten, sat and goggled at the scene.

It was only about fifteen seconds actually before Sister O'Neill bore down on them and escorted them both outside, but it more than made up for a rather routine week.

Poor Mrs Ford was very subdued all the rest of that day, sitting there with bits of blue glitter and eyelash all down her face and not bothering to wipe them away.

As it was my last day, I never found out any more details, but I'd love to have known who visited her the next day.

You needn't write back to this because I'll be seeing you in a week or so. Please can you get some stuff from work so that you can do my hair black properly. I want to change my image and be all dark and dramatic when I come back here. (I bet as soon as I've done it I'll discover that he *only likes blondes.)*

Love, Emma xxx

Southpark General
25th June

Dear Martin,
I'll be seeing you in a few days so all my news can wait until then. I'm a bit bewildered by your last letter – I honestly didn't mean to sound 'cold' in my *last one. Maybe I did waffle on a bit about hospital happenings and didn't mention 'us' very much, but I've said before that I think we should stay off the passionate stuff.*

Anyway, I can't wait to see you and everyone at home – also look round your new garage. I hope you'll be able to meet me at the station because I'll have a load of stuff with me. Mostly it's text books I've got to get through before my next ward but there'll be the odd suitcase of dirty washing too – and *my complete uniform which Mum has insisted I bring home and dress up in. I think she wants to parade me in front of the neighbours in it.*

I should be on the train that arrives at noon on

Sunday, but I'll ring you if anything happens and I miss it.

Lots of love, Emma xxx

18 Colleton Avenue,
Westerley
1st July

Dear Bev,
Hi! Here I am safely installed in my little pink bedroom at home, amazed to find that I really miss everyone back at the hospital. Thought I'd be pleased to get away – and I was – but am now suffering definite pangs of hospital sickness.

Think it's because of all the girls and the laughs we've had. Being an only child I've really enjoyed having lots of people around me; it's a bit like I imagine a boarding school would be. By the way, Mum says if we can get our holidays at the same time you must come home with me next time. I know you've got aunties and stuff in this country but I bet you'd enjoy staying here. There are sheep *nearby; you'd really feel at home.*

How is everyone? Jeremy, Cathy, Nicola, Sally – and dear Immo, of course? Thought of any good ideas to plague her? Did you hear that Daddy was whisking her off to the Seychelles for two weeks? Bet she comes back all golden like a suntan oil advert with not a peeled nose or a freckle in sight.

Must admit it's lovely being waited on. Mum and Dad are making a big fuss of me; to hear them talk you'd think I was sustaining the health service single-handed. They keep talking about 'calls of duty' and 'high-minded devotion' – stuff like that. I don't think it's occurred to them that I'm actually enjoying nursing.

Martin is being a bit of a pain, but I'll tell you more about that when I come back. My friends are the same as ever; did I tell you about the one called Julie? She thinks nursing is a cross between waitressing and cleaning lavatories; someone asked me a perfectly normal question about bed-bathing and she shuddered delicately and said, 'I don't know how you could*!' It's just as well she doesn't know what else we have to do!*

Actually, she's the one that my friend Avril wrote and told me was after Martin, and now that I'm home I can see that she obviously is*. She's doing the 'hysterical at his jokes' and 'flicking imaginary dust from lapels' routine on every possible occasion. When I mentioned to him that Julie fancied him, though, he just laughed and said not to be silly and surely I wasn't jealous?*

I'm not really. At least, I don't think I am.

What ward are you on next? I've forgotten. I'm on Maternity and I'm quite looking forward to it though I've never as much as picked a baby up before. That doll in the training school was quite easy to manage, but I've got a feeling that they're not really quite as quiet and cooperative as that. I've brought loads of books home with me and am swotting up on Care of the Newborn*.*

I didn't hear from Jon before I left. I've been

wondering whether to write to him – would that be a bit pushy, d'you think? Perhaps I'll just send a postcard or something.

See you soon. Love to everyone at the hospital and love to you,

from Emma xxx

Diary

10th July
My last night at home for six months or so. I don't start on Maternity until Monday but I'm going back a couple of days early to get sorted out and try and get some studying

done. I've tried to read at home but find it very difficult to put my mind to anything; if I *do* sit down at the dining-room table, out of the corner of my eye I can see Mum walking around on tiptoe whispering loudly that 'she won't speak to me because she knows it will disturb me'.

I think that once I get back to the busy hospital atmosphere it'll be easier to concentrate, daft though that sounds.

Martin was awful last night. I said I couldn't see him tonight so he made a big thing of making yesterday 'an evening to remember'. Trouble was, he wanted to remember it quite differently from the way I did.

He took me for a meal, which was lovely, and he'd borrowed a car from the garage to take me in. Snag: the car was equipped with one of those buttons that you press to make the front seats go down flat.

Needless to say, on the way home he stopped the car and we had to see how it worked. One minute I was quietly sitting there minding my own business and the next I was flat on my back.

'Eek! I said, scrabbling about like an upturned crab.

'What's the matter,' he said, 'don't you want to say goodbye properly?'

Well, no, I didn't – not if properly meant *that* – and I told him so. I don't think I was being prudish or anything. I know we've done more than just kissing in the past but that was ages ago when I was at home and all terribly keen on him. We just don't have that sort of relationship any more.

I started giggling – I felt so silly lying there flat on my back in a borrowed car with Martin doing the passionate seducer bit – and after a minute he pushed the 'up' button and drove on. I think he was as relieved as I was, if the truth be known.

'Course, I had about a million kisses to endure, and lots of promises that he would be faithful and pleas that I would, too. I didn't commit myself!

I sometimes think that if he wasn't quite so keen, I'd be a lot keener, but that's the way it always goes. When you're keen on them, they never like you.

Which brings me back to Luke, I suppose. I had a letter from Bev but she didn't say anything about him. Really scared that I'll get back and find that he and Nicola are back together. It's silly and immature of me, I know.

Wonder if Nicola's finished my birth chart? Now that I'm almost there I can't wait to hear what's been happening while I've been away.

Chapter six

Southpark General
20th July

Dear Mum and Dad,
After swotting up on newborn babies, I got back to find myself assigned to an orthopaedic ward (bones!) which was a bit of a blow. Apparently another student nurse, Sonia, had been due to come on here but failed her last block so didn't return to the hospital after her holidays, and then two of the regular orthopaedic nurses were ill, so they asked me to change. I don't mind too much because Beverley is also on this ward with me, so we've been having quite a few laughs.

The first laugh turned out to be the Sister, who's about a year off retiring age and quite a dear old hen. A hen, in fact, is just what she's like because she makes this funny clucking noise in her throat all the time. She obviously doesn't know she's doing it but it's a great alarm system; if you're having a crafty cup of tea in the sluice room and you hear a 'cluck cluck' coming down the ward, you know to sling your tea in the sink and start crashing the bedpans around busily.

This is a men's ward and they mostly have things like broken legs and arms, though there are some who are in the middle of a series of operations to correct different bone deformities. Because they're not actually ill they're a jolly lot, always community singing (usually rude stuff) – though Sister nearly goes mad to stop them whenever there are consultants around.

We've got a very high and mighty consultant for this ward: Sir Clifton Hillard, who's about twice removed from God. We had a visitation from him the second day I was on the ward and Sister got so agitated trying to get the ward in order for him that she practically clucked herself to death. Sir Clifton approached the bed of this very dour old stick by the name of Mr Wakeman, asking in his very plummy condescending voice:

'And how are we, today?'

The old boy scowled at him. 'No better for seeing you!' he snarled.

Sister almost laid an egg.

I quite often have to get patients ready for surgery now. I have a staff nurse supervising me or one of the clinical teachers comes in from the school, and we go through the pre-operation routine together and then I take the patient down to the theatre on a trolley. I quite enjoy doing this because they are usually a bit nervous and glad to have someone they know around. Even the crabby old ones like Mr Wakeman have been known to want their hands held as they are wheeled through the double doors into the theatre.

We student nurses don't get round to doing theatre duty until the third year. I'm quite looking *forward to it as it looks so high-powered and important in there – lots of green-gowned and masked figures scurrying about, massive machinery and huge arc lamps.*

Write soon. I love hearing all the little bits of gossip from home.

Love, Emma xxx

Southpark General
4th August

Dear Avril,

My hair colour is a hit; everyone likes it. I do *feel different being darker, more vital and dramatic or something (don't laugh).*

I've seen Luke! I wasn't expecting to see him at all on this ward because I knew that he and Jeremy had done orthopaedics, so it was a real shock when he walked in yesterday.

I'd just started to bandage an abrasion on the wrist of this old chap by the name of Mr Wakeman and he was moaning away and saying that they shouldn't let ninnies and children practise on him (don't know which I was) and why couldn't he have a 'proper' nurse, when in came Luke.

Well, I was so startled that I jumped about a foot in the air and dropped the bandage. Mr Wakeman said loudly: 'Oh, it's your young man, is it? No wonder your mind's not on the job!' When I looked round for the bandage it had gone right across the floor, unrolling itself as it went, and ended up almost at Luke's feet. Oh, the shame of it!

I felt like diving under the nearest bed but I mustered what dignity I had left and went across the ward to him. He bent down to retrieve one end and handed it to me saying, 'Yours, I believe.' Ooh, he's got these lovely eyes which in close-up are a real dark blue. I was quite overcome.

As I stood there holding yards of bandage and feeling silly, Sister clucked up.

'Nurse!' she said. 'Did I just see that bandage rolling across the floor?'

'Yes, Sister.'

'I trust you aren't going to put it on the patient now. Cluck cluck.'

'No, Sister,' (in shocked voice) 'because of the cross-infection.'

'Quite.'

I scurried back to Mr Wakeman and he said loudly: 'Shouldn't be allowed. Carrying on with half the hospital while patients are dying all around.'

I bet Luke heard, too.

I found out from Beverley later that he'd gone in to see how a particular patient of his (he'd done a case history on him) was doing. Bev is still seeing Jeremy quite regularly, though only once or twice a week at the moment because they both (like the rest of us) have so much studying to do.

I do a spell of night duty soon. Not looking forward to it, as they say you take really ages to get into the swing of sleeping days and being up nights;

you have permanent jet-lag for days. Just as you do get used to it, you're changed back again. At least the wards will be quieter at night so that I can get some reading done. Hope *they will be, anyway.*

Had an amazing birth chart cast for me by Nicola. I can't tell you all the things – just that you're extremely lucky to have a wonderful, versatile, generous, outgoing and truly charming friend like me. I expect you know that already, though. Seriously, I must try and chat her up to do one for you, because it's quite uncannily accurate (apart from the nasty bits).

6th August – coffee time
Stop press. *The most gorgeous guy has been delivered to our ward. He's a window cleaner who fell off his ladder and broke his ankle. The porter just wheeled him up on a trolley; I was sorting the linen cupboard and Beverley was filling water jugs. Sister said:*

'Cluck cluck. . . would one of you student nurses get Mr Bradley into bed, please?' And Bev and I just glanced over – did a double-take – and rushed for the trolley together.

'I'll do it,' I said to Bev, 'you carry on with the jugs.'

'No, I'll do it. You carry on with the linen cupboard. You make such a lovely job of it.'

'But no one fills up water jugs quite like you!'

She rolled her eyes. 'OK,' she said, 'but bags I the next beaut.'

Luckily Mr Bradley (first names Gerald

Michael) was still groggy from the anaesthetic so didn't hear any of this. I got him into bed (and no, I didn't have to undress him because he'd come up from recovery room and already had hospital pyjamas on), made a chart up, saw to his locker and water and pulled the curtains round him so that he could rest a bit longer (also so that Beverley wouldn't be able to see him).

He's really dishy. It's against all the rules, of course, to chat up patients, but who's to know if you fancy them? Besides, I feel I need a bit of sunshine in my life, because it doesn't look as if Luke is interested in me. It's just as well, really, because if he was *I don't think I could have any sort of casual fling with him. It would more than likely be the sort of relationship that would knock all my studying on the head and leave me in a permanently soppy state.*

Must go back now and see if Mr Bradley needs anything. No wonder Bev said she'd take a late coffee break – she's probably flapping round his bed right now.

Love, Emma xxx

PS Have a good time at Angela's party. Hope you manage to get off with Paul.

Southpark General
17th August

Dear Martin,
Your letter came as quite a shock considering all the

little talks we had and all the things I said about not wanting to get serious about you (or anyone). I really thought we understood each other.

Honestly, Martin, I don't think it would be a good idea to get engaged at Christmas. An engagement is supposed to be used for getting to know each other better and we can hardly do that when we're at opposite ends of the country. I know how you feel and I appreciate all the thinking you must have done before asking me, but I really don't think it's on. Let's just stay friends for now and see what happens.

You asked me about the babies, but when I got back I found that my schedule had been changed and that I was on Orthopaedic. I'm quite enjoying it, though, as Beverley is with me.

We get all sorts of funny cases in here (I don't think the patients think they're very funny, mind you). We've got a man who tripped over his dog and broke his leg, another who had a row with his wife and fell down the stairs (we think she pushed him) and a window cleaner who fell off his ladder.

I've been looking after a ten-year-old this week who's got a broken leg that won't mend. He should really be in a children's ward but Sir Clifton Hillard (posh bone specialist) wants to keep a special eye on him. This little boy, whose name is Rowan, keeps asking questions about what's going on in the ward. Well, you can imagine, can't you?

'What's that bloke having done to him?' he said today when someone was being prepared for an operation.

I explained and then he said loudly: 'Suppose he don't wake up afterwards?'

'Of course *he will,' I said in my best nurselike reassuring manner.*

'I shouldn't bank on it, he don't look too good to me,' he said darkly, then he cheered up and said: 'Can I have his grapes if he don't?'

Avril said you've all been invited to a really swish eighteenth birthday party at Angela's dad's club. Lucky lot; I wish I could go. There's no chance that I'll be able to join you, though, because as well as all the studying I've got to do, I start on night duty next week, so I won't know whether I'm coming or going.

Enjoy yourself, anyway. Don't do anything naughty!

Lots of love, Emma xxx

Diary

26th August
This is my third night of Nights. The hospital is quite different: very quiet and shadowy and a bit eerie. There's fewer staff around, too, usually just me and a staff nurse on the ward with a Sister hovering between us and the female orthopaedic. She is more often in there because they have a very modern kitchen unit and she cooks herself midnight feasts.

The staff nurse with me is a black girl called

Josie, really nice and friendly. She leaves me studying while she does most of the checking of patients – she says she'd fall asleep if she didn't keep on the move. The only time we *are* busy is from five o'clock onwards when we have to wake the patients up and wash them ready for the day staff to take over. They don't take very kindly to being woken at five, either!

My last week on days was really enjoyable as Gerald, window cleaner, was up and hobbling about and chatting me up quite a bit. I've not been paying him any more attention than any of the other patients (at least, I don't think I have) but it's just been nice to have someone to look forward to seeing; I've worn make-up every single day since he came in!

He's quite mobile now and will be going out at the end of the week, and I reckon we'll all miss him. He's so nice and such a laugh; he can even charm Sister off her perch.

He says he can never go to sleep before the small hours so last night he joined me and Josie for a cup of tea in the sluice room. We were all laughing about something he was telling us – one of the usual window cleaner's tales about cleaning a bathroom window with a naked woman inside – when there was a tap at the door. Josie had just done a round of the patients and they were all asleep, so we thought it was Sister – or worse. The door opened and it was *Jon*, all in police uniform and looking quite dashing.

I was really surprised; I haven't seen a glimpse of him since before I went home.

'Hello, sweetheart!' he said to me. 'Wondered when I'd find you again.'

'Would you like a cup of tea?' I said, all other small talk failing me.

He said he would and Josie disappeared back on to the ward, leaving me with the two of them!

Jon said he'd been on night duty for some time and as the hospital was on his beat he usually popped in for a cup of tea about this time. He reckoned that Women's Medical was the best, as they did a nice line in cheese on toast in there.

I assured him that there was no chance of *me* making him cheese on toast, but he didn't seem too put out.

'Thought I might find you on night duty one day,' he said, 'that's why I've been doing my rounds of the wards.'

After a minute or two of this I began to feel really awkward; I didn't know how to behave with either of them and there was a distinct possibility that Sister would come by and discover me. Couldn't help wishing that if anyone had to see me being chatted up by two guys it would be Luke!

So I made my excuses and scurried back to the ward, Jon just saying that he'd 'See me around'. Ha! I know from experience exactly

August
26 Wednesday 238 127
...Have been scribbling all this down while Jose
it lunch even though it's one o'clock in the
been over to talk to me. "Back to bed, Mr.
more tea tonight!" — "I don't want tea," he
ask you out". (FLABBERGASTED SILENCE from me!!!)
to go out with patients," I said at last.
"In two days I won't be a patient, how about then
I said I'd let him know.. but really I know already —
I'M GOING — of course ... I'M GOING!!!
27 Thursday 239 126
31st AUGUST.
Have just had the most fantastic evening in spite of what happened at the end of it. He (GERALD) took me to a restaurant with a dance
floor and a cabaret. We have a beautiful meal (roast duck), danced, laughed
at the cabaret, and danced some more. It was FABULOUS — just what I
fondly imagined I'd be doing every single weekend when I was in LONDON!
I'd just about decided to fall WHOLLY in love with him when he said:
"I'm pleased you came because I really wanted to thank you properly for
looking after me."
28 Friday 240 125
"ALL PART OF THE SERVICE!!!"
"No, really. Sonia and I are really greatful. I might
have had to be wheeled down the aisle if it hadn't been for you."
"Wheeled down the aisle?" I echoed faintly.
"Yup! Only a month to go now. Sonia said I should be sure to take you out
and thank you properly."
"How nice of
I said politely." Er... I don't remember anyone
one like a fiancée anyway."
abroad for a year on an exchange visit.
"Well, congratulations!" I said
Moon rises 05 36 Moon sets

what *that* means. Wonder why he even bothered to look for me.

Later
Have been scribbling all this down while Josie is at lunch (they still call it lunch even though it's one o'clock in the morning). Gerald has just been over to talk to me.

'Back to bed, Mr Bradley,' I said. 'There's no more tea tonight.'

'I don't want tea,' he said, 'I want to ask you out.'

Flabbergasted silence from me. 'I. . . I'm not allowed to go out with patients,' I said at last.

'In two days I won't be a patient, how about then?'

I said I'd let him know, but really I know already. I'm going – *of course* I'm going!

31st August
Have just had the most fantastic evening in spite of what happened at the end of it. He (Gerald) took me to a restaurant with a dance floor and a cabaret. We had a beautiful meal (roast duck), danced, laughed at the cabaret and danced some more. It was fabulous – just what I fondly imagined I'd be doing every single weekend when I was in London!

I'd just about decided to fall madly in love with him when he said: 'I'm pleased you came because I really wanted to thank you properly for looking after me.'

'All part of the service!'

'No, really. Sonia and I are really grateful. I might have had to be wheeled down the aisle if it hadn't been for you.'

'Wheeled down the aisle?' I echoed faintly.

'Yup. Only a month to go now. Sonia said I should be sure to take you out and thank you properly.'

'How nice of Sonia,' I said politely. 'Er. . . I don't remember anyone coming to visit you – no one like a fiancée, anyway.'

'Oh, she's been abroad for a year on an exchange visit. She's a teacher.'

'Well, congratulations!' I said with false heartiness. 'I didn't realize!'

What a *choke*. I suppose there's always the faint hope that Sonia will decide to stay exchanged. Not very likely, though.

It's back to gazing at Luke from afar, then.

Whilst I'm writing about love and such matters – I haven't heard a word from Martin since my letter turning him down, and I usually get about three letters from him to every one of mine. I bet I've really offended him now. What else could I say, though? Really feel quite fed up with the opposite sex at the moment.

Chapter seven

Southpark General
Monday 31st August

Dear Mum and Dad,
My last week on Orthopaedic. I'm back in school next week with an exam at the end of it and then I've got nearly a week off.

Won't be able to make it home. Apart from the train fare I've so much reading to do that I'll probably just sit around here and get on with it. Bev's week falls with mine so perhaps we'll go out for the day or something.

You're not thinking of taking a lodger, are you? I had an awful dream last night in which I came home and went up to my room and it wasn't mine. *Apart from the wallpaper and carpet and stuff even the shape had changed and there were all strange posters and photos on the walls, and someone was in my bed! Sounds funny now but it was really quite scary and horrible. Don't let anyone else have it, will you?!*

Sorry to hear about your toe, but honestly, Mum, it's no use asking me for advice – I've only been on the ward for seven weeks and even the WI lady who brings the teas round the ward knows more about bones than I do. If it still hurts I should go and see Dr Walmsey – though there's not a lot they can do if it is broken; with toes I think you just have to leave them to get on with it.

I survived night duty quite well and eventually got used to sleeping during the day. Sheer tiredness makes you drop off in the end, though Bev swears that she didn't sleep at all *and worked out that at the end of her week of Nights she had been awake for 168 hours! Didn't believe a word of it. Some of us adjusted to a different sleeping pattern more easily than others, of course, and I suppose I was one of the lucky ones. Just as well because from now all the spells on different wards will contain some night duty.*

Old Mr Wakeman, our longest-stay patient, was discharged yesterday. Although he never stopped moaning about the hospital, the food, the treatment and the nurses (especially me) I think he was sorry to leave; Sister swore that she saw tears in his eyes. It's quite strange in here now with no one cursing and shouting: 'This tea's like gnats' pee!' or (weakly) 'Nurse, I think I'm slipping away.'

He's gone back to one room at the top of an old unheated house with no family and no one to look after him. Terrible, really.

I still find it very difficult not to get involved with people's problems – they say that it's ages before you become really detached. Have been feeling morbid for the past few days because we had a road accident victim die on us just when we thought he was making a complete recovery. He was exactly my age, too.

Oh dear, I don't want to depress you! There are lots of nice things happening as well – one chap here has made the progression from wheelchair through operations to a walking frame, then crutches, and last week he took his very first steps unaided. The whole ward (those that could get up, anyway) gave him a standing ovation when he walked unsteadily through the doors. Felt all tearful!

Love, Emma xxx

Southpark General
11th September

Dear Avril,
I'm so blooming cheesed off I could SPIT! I hate everyone!

Not you. I do appreciate being told. I'd never have forgiven you if you'd just let me go on thinking that everything was just the same.

Well! I could hardly believe my eyes when I read your letter. The thing is, you didn't know that in his last letter to me Martin actually proposed – wanted me to get engaged at Christmas! What d'you think of that? Now, a couple of weeks later, you say he was at Angela's party with Julie and took her home afterwards!

Really, I feel ever so bitter about it. I mean, it was him all along who wanted to keep things going between us, not me. I tried to cool it down – but at the same time I must admit that it was nice having him there wanting me. Now, without even a 'by your leave', he goes off with Julie. I think he might have had the decency to tell me himself, don't you?

I'm going to leave it a week or two and see if he writes and tells me what's happened, then take it from there. If he doesn't write I think I might write to him, perhaps saying that I've been thinking things over and have decided I will *get engaged to him at Christmas. Let him wriggle out of that one!*

My success with the opposite sex must be at an all-time low. And there was me happily thinking that I only had to don a pair of black stockings for them all to come running. You remember the good-looking window cleaner patient we had? Well, he asked me out, and I went, only to find that it was just a 'thank you' and that he was getting married next month! Also, Jon came in one night when I was on Nights but hasn't been back since – and I haven't even glimpsed *Luke.*

Bev and I tried to arrange a party in the sitting room of the nurses' home but on the Saturday we tentatively arranged it for, half of our intake were going to be on Nights and the other half were on holiday. So we cancelled it.

I'm fed up! I bet I'm going to turn into one of those nasty, crabby old Sisters who terrorize the student nurses. I can feel it creeping up on me right now.

You must write and tell me if they've been seen together since (Martin and Julie, I mean) and what they looked like (in love? passionate? just good friends?), also if you've had any reaction from anyone else. Ooh, I'm so mad! Isn't that typical – declaring his love one minute and whisking off with the first girl who gives him the eye the next! Just wish I was at home so I could tell them what I think of them.

I'll have to stop writing about them or this pen will catch fire. I'll tell you what I've been doing lately.

Well, I'm off the ward and am back in school for two weeks. Some of it has been spent working out ways in which we can help patients who've lost the use of their legs, either temporarily or permanently, and to give us the feel of what it would be like we were taken in groups of three to a busy shopping area, one of us on crutches, one in a wheelchair and one pushing.

Well! Bev wanted to be the first in a wheelchair so I had to push, and Cathy (she's the cockney one) was on crutches. We practised for a bit down an alleyway then emerged, giggling all over the place.

Bev had a rug over her knees so that no one could see what sort of disablement she had but I'm sure no one was fooled for a minute because she kept saying 'Faster, faster!' and 'Wheee!' whenever we went down slopes, and I was bright red with embarrassment.

Cathy was hobbling along saying 'Ah ha, me hearties' and doing a fair impersonation of Long John Silver. Altogether I think we must have looked a pretty unlikely trio.

The worst bit was when Bev said she wanted to

go in a bank (we were told to see what sort of facilities for the disabled there were) so she made me go ahead and ask the manager.

'I've got a disabled friend outside who'd like to come in and do some business,' I said all stuttery and shame-faced, and he was so charming and helpful that I felt even worse. He rushed out to her with a wooden ramp so that the wheelchair could come up the steps and then brought out a special table to go over the wheelchair arms so that she could write her cheque. She accepted all this fuss quite calmly – I wouldn't have minded so much but she didn't even bank with them! When we got out she wanted to repeat the whole procedure at another bank with me in the chair, but I wasn't having it!

We did change over a bit later. We went into an alleyway, having just passed a bus queue with Bev in the chair and Cathy on crutches, then came out of the alleyway with me in the chair and Bev on crutches. When we passed the bus queue you should have seen the looks we got! They obviously thought it was some nasty new teenage kick.

Write soon. Don't spare me a thing – never mind about the three wise monkeys.

Love, Emma xxx

Southpark General
18th September

Dear Martin,

It's been several weeks since I heard from you but I have *heard from Avril so I know what's going on.*

I think you're a real pig not to write and tell me that you're going out with Julie. Avril told me that you were with her at Angela's party and also that you've been seen with her since, so don't try to deny it.

I'm really hurt – especially so as in your last letter you actually asked me to marry you! Some devotion that was! I know I said I didn't want to, but are your feelings really that shallow that you can turn them on to someone else so quickly?

I would have thought that we were friendly enough, had been through enough together, for us to be truthful with each other. It's not very nice to be away from home and have your best friend write and say that your boyfriend is going out with the town scrubber. I said *she was out to get you and that's what she's obviously done.*

Well, good luck to the both of you. You deserve each other.

Emma

Diary

24th September
Have been doing a lot of thinking and now feel absolutely terrible about the letter I sent to Martin. I shouldn't have said what I did (actually called her a scrubber, too) but I was so miserable a couple of days ago and I just

sat brooding about what had happened and what a fool I felt and before I knew it, it was written. Most of the depression was brought about because my period was due and, as usual, things seemed ten times worse than they really were. Perhaps there should be an addition to that saying about never writing a letter in anger – never write a letter in anger or when you've got pre-menstrual tension, perhaps.

Anyway, I can see now what a total hypocrite I've been. I said something about us being truthful to each other but I haven't been truthful to him. I've fancied Luke for ages *and* I've been out with Jon and Gerald and haven't said a word about them.

I suppose I have tried to be honest. I did say early on that I didn't feel we should try and remain faithful to each other, but he wouldn't accept it.

I think what I feel badly about is the loss of face at home; there was I all fully confident of Martin's feelings for me, thinking that there was a little vacuum in his (and everyone else's) life that I could refill when and if I felt like it, and now I've got to face up to the fact that life at home has moved on without me.

So. . . I'll really have to write to Martin again asking him to burn my last letter. God help me if he's already shown Julie the bit about her being a scrubber – she'll be on her way to do me over.

RADIO CAROLINE
TAL.
Bell

28th September
Haven't yet got up the nerve to write to Martin again, and haven't heard from him, either.

Passed my last (Orthopaedic) block OK. Everyone says Maternity is pretty stiff so I really must try and keep my mind off my personal problems and get some hard studying done.

This is supposed to be my week off; I've spent most of it writing up my notes so that they're readable, filing stuff away in the right places and trying to bring my room into some sort of order. I've also replenished my box of goodies in the kitchen, done loads of washing and *slept*.

Since I've been at the hospital the days have gone by so fast – in her last letter Mum was talking about Christmas – it doesn't bear thinking about. Wish something wonderful and exciting would happen to brighten things up. Something *romantic* and wonderful and exciting, preferably.

Southpark General
1st October

Dear Martin,
I've been feeling terrible ever since I wrote to you, and now that I think about what I said I know how selfish and nasty I must have sounded.

Sorry. Obviously you couldn't help falling for

Julie any more than I *could have done if it had happened to me. I think the trouble was I thought it* was *going to happen to me, that's why it was such a bombshell when you turned the tables.*

Anyway, I hope you'll forgive me for writing as I did; I take back everything I said.

Write soon and say that we can still be friends.

Emma xxx

Chapter eight

Southpark General
Monday 5th October

Dear Mum and Dad,
I started here on Maternity – or Obstetrics as it should be called – last Monday and have really been enjoying it. This six weeks is only supposed to be a very general clinical experience which will take in all the different departments, and we come back to do eight weeks more specialized training at the end of our three years.

We go all over the whole Maternity block starting at the beginning which is the booking-in clinic, where women come from ten weeks' pregnant, then on to the ante-natal wards (some women are in for the full nine months), reception (where they arrive when they're in labour), labour wards, progress wards, theatres and then post-natal wards when they've got the babies. Also premature baby unit and post-natal clinic. There's probably somewhere I've forgotten but you can see what a lot there is to get through.

At the moment I'm in the booking-in clinic with a staff nurse and we have to take down hundreds of details from each new patient, then the staff nurse looks at how she's shaping up, after which she's laid out like a fish on a slab (the patient, not staff nurse) for the doctor to come and lay his cold hands on her. It's quite interesting, as all the patients seem to want to chat and be friendly and most are really pleased to be there. One wasn't today, actually. She was having her eighth *baby; came in with a brood of children who crawled up the curtains, over the weighing scales and into the cupboards. Told me gloomily that if she could find out what was causing them she'd stop!*

I've booked in two unmarried girls; one was only sixteen. Felt sorry for her but she wanted none of it, said she'd only done it so that the council would provide her with a flat and she could get away from home.

Leaving nursing aside for the moment; I'd better tell you this before you see Martin around the place with Another Woman and have a fit. I've broken up with him and he's now going out with Julie. I know you'll be upset, Mum, I know you like him a lot, but I never really did think it would come to anything with us being all this distance apart. I'm sure it's for the best.

Write soon!

Love, Emma xxx

PS Don't be embarrassed when you see him will you? I mean, don't cut him dead or anything, even if she is with him.

Southpark General
20th October

Dear Avril,
Thanks for your two letters; I feel happier now. Well, a bit!

I've heard from Martin at last. It was a nice 'no hard feelings' sort of letter in which he said he just suddenly fancied Julie like mad, didn't know what hit him (her boobs in that push-up bra, perhaps?) and hoped we could all be friends. Feel a lot better since he wrote; I'd been feeling terrible about the nasty things I said to him in my letter.

Oh – nearly forgot! Really pleased that you're going out with Paul at last, you lucky thing. I don't know how you do it, you always *manage to get off with the guy you fancy. Makes me sick.*

I've at last got some chance of meeting up with Luke again, but knowing me I shall probably make a muck up of it. There's a Hallowe'en party here in the social club on the thirty-first and everyone's *going. There have been parties and dances in the social club before and they've been terrible. Bev and I went to one a couple of weeks ago and there must have been all of four people there (including us). But this, they say, is traditionally a fantastic evening. Everyone makes a special effort with masks and stuff and even those who are on duty manage to put in an appearance. So, here's hoping that something – anything – will happen.*

Had a bit of a traumatic day today. God, if it was traumatic for me I don't know what Mrs Ditcham would call it. She is in the long-stay ante-

natal ward (in her own room, just off it, actually, as she's supposed to rest a lot). Why? Because she's had seven miscarriages, poor thing. Isn't that awful?

She's very nice, early thirties, and always desperate for someone to chat to, so I've been spending some time with her every day this week. Have got to know her quite well – she even invited me to come back at visiting time to meet her husband. She's been in seven months now and only this morning said something about 'So far so good, I've never got this far before'.

I took her in a cup of tea this afternoon and we were talking about our ambitions and how they change over the years. Mine was to pass my finals and make a good nurse and hers was to push a pram down the street with her own baby in it. She stretched over to put her cup of tea back on her locker then clutched herself and said: 'My waters have gone!'

Instant panic whilst trying to appear instantly competent. She started crying loudly, saying that it was 'too soon' and she was going to lose another baby and I dashed outside and rang immediately for the nearest doctor to come.

Sister came in, then Staff, and tried to calm her down, but she'd started to have pains almost immediately so they knew it was the real thing. The doctor came, gave her a brisk once-over and said she was to be taken down to the labour ward straight away. I felt so sorry for her; she was really frightened. (So was I.)

The porter wheeled her bed down and I went with her. I stayed there for a while, knowing that we weren't very busy upstairs, and the pains got worse and doctors dashed about and then she was wired up to a big machine on which you could hear the baby's heartbeat, etc. Her face when she could hear that it was still alive was lovely to see!

Eventually I had to go back to my ward, but I went down in my teabreak and *when I went off duty, only to be told that she was still in strong labour.*

I cooked myself some food which I couldn't eat and then went over again; I knew I wouldn't have been able to sleep otherwise. The same Sister was on duty in the labour ward and she laughed when she saw me. I knew then that it was all right.

'She had a girl!' she said. 'Both doing well.'

I was so relieved I came over all peculiar and had to sit down. Apparently the baby was small, only five pounds, but quite healthy. It had gone up to the premature baby unit so I couldn't see it. I couldn't see her, either, because she was asleep, but I peeped into the recovery room and there was a bottle of champagne, an enormous bouquet of flowers and a big teddy on the locker.

'As you can see, her husband's been,' Sister said, looking in over my shoulder.

I must go and get her a card tomorrow. It's the first baby I've been personally involved in; feel so chuffed that I can't sleep!

22nd October

Stop press! *Have just had a letter from* Julie! *To be fair, it's quite a nice letter, though written on scented pink paper. She says she didn't mean it to happen (ha!), hopes I'm not too upset and wants us still to be friends. I'm not half as worried about it as she seems to think I am, of course. The whole business seems silly now and Martin seems a million miles and another lifestyle away.*

Write soon and tell me more about Paul. Wish me luck at the Hallowe'en do.

Love, Emma xxx

Southpark General
24th October

Dear Julie,

Thank you for your letter and please don't feel guilty for another minute.

I knew quite well that Martin and I wouldn't survive being apart for three years and what has happened was inevitable, really, so don't worry about it any more.

I don't want you to think that I'm pining away here – far from it. I'm very busy and happy and there's always a lot going on. We've got a hospital dance next Saturday for Hallowe'en, for instance. I've been to loads of dances at the social club before, of course, and they're always a riot, but this one is by tradition something special. Most of us are making our own masks. There will be some ghosts by courtesy of the hospital linen cupboards and the skeletons from the medical school usually put in an appearance. Just about all the hospital staff will be there.

So, no hard feelings on either side, then. I expect I'll see you all when I come home at Christmas.

Until then,

Best wishes, Emma

Diary

26th October
Have been on the post-natal ward all week. There's a lovely atmosphere up here; the mums are all sitting up looking pleased with themselves, there are lots of flowers around, and babies, of course, and a general air of achievement hangs over everything.

There are side wards, for those women who have had stillbirths or babies born handicapped, but I have nothing to do with them at the moment. All I do is wheel the babies backwards and forwards from the wards to the nursery, get the bottles for the mums that want them at feeding times and haul nappies around (clean and otherwise). I haven't even seen a baby born yet, but I don't know whether that's deliberate on their part or not. I was all due to see one when I was helping on the progress ward but then the birth turned out to be complicated and the mother was rushed off to theatre. I'm not really in too much of a rush to see a birth; I'm a bit apprehensive about it – just as I am about seeing any surgery. I'd hate to disgrace myself.

Mrs Ditcham is up here – a new, slim, beaming Mrs Ditcham. Baby Gemma is still up in the prem. unit so she spends most of her days up there watching her. She said she *has* to keep going up there just to convince herself she's really got a baby at last.

Lots of preparations going on for the Hallowe'en do. Bev is wearing her flapper's dress and has made a mask to match it, with fringes. As I don't seem to have anything madly exciting in my wardrobe (and can't afford to buy anything) I'm just wearing my black silky dress and am making a glamorous (hopefully) mask out of cardboard, black velvet and sequins.

The cardboard is from an empty box I found on the ward so inside my mask it says 'Disposable gloves for obstetric use'. Must take care that no one sees the inside!

Nicola is going as a witch's cat in furry gloves and pussycat mask with whiskers; at least two are going in sheets as ghosts. Don't know what Imogen is going as, but she's looking very smug whenever it's mentioned.

1st November

Have been floating about blissfully all day. The Hallowe'en party was fantastic – and so was Luke.

To start with, the whole place was done up beautifully with balloons, fairy lights, pumpkins with candles inside and all the Hallowe'en gear. Everyone was dressed up, or at least had masks on and Imogen had hired a full Madame de Pompadour outfit with diamond-encrusted lace everywhere and foot-high hairdo, face patches and mask on a stick. She looked *awful*, really overdone. She's so thin that the dress seemed to be wearing her!

Anyway, about ten o'clock I'd eaten, danced a bit and done all the apple-bobbing games and was beginning to feel slightly desperate because there was no sign of Luke. Then, about ten-fifteen, in came four white-gowned figures wearing surgical masks – the only slight effort they'd made was to put a couple of cut-out stars and moons on to them. Once they got nearer I knew one was him; there was no mistaking those eyes, even muffled in white.

'Are you supposed to be anyone in particular?' he asked.

'Only me.' I nodded towards Imogen. 'Someone else had already bought up the hire shop,' I added.

'You'll do fine as you,' he said, and we started dancing. It was as easy as that.

Honestly, I don't know how I ever could

have thought that I hated him. Well, I didn't really, did I? He's so nice, kind and funny. After an hour or so of dancing and talking I began to feel quite light-headed – and I knew it wasn't the non-alcoholic punch they were serving.

At midnight they announced that we should unmask.

'Suppose I'm not who you think I am?' I said. I was fishing, of course, but I couldn't help it.

'I know exactly who you are,' he said.

So then we took our masks off and all the lights went out and he put his arms round me and kissed me.

When the kiss was over and the lights went on again we stood, him still with his arms

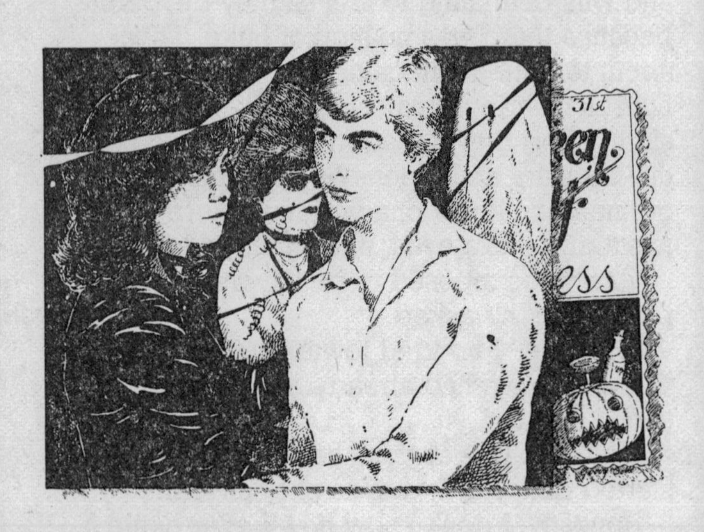

round me, just looking at each other. It was a strange, emotional moment and I felt so funny inside, just as if I couldn't breathe. We gazed and gazed and just when I felt that I couldn't bear it another second and I'd have to look away, or speak, just to break the tension, Jeremy and Bev came up and started chatting.

When I close my eyes and think about it now, I can bring back that moment vividly. I *have* been bringing it back vividly, in fact, all day.

When he walked me back to the nurses' home he kissed me again and said: 'I'll see you soon, won't I?' and I said, 'Yes, please.'

All I want to know now is, how soon is *soon*.

Chapter nine

Southpark General
Sunday 8th November

Dear Mum and Dad,
Sorry if this letter is later than usual; I've been up to my eyes in babies.

Well, you asked me about the Hallowe'en dance – yes, it was great and, yes, Mum, I did *meet someone nice. Trouble is, I haven't heard from him since. It's not long, I suppose. Perhaps he'll get in touch this week.*

I finished on Obstetrics on Friday. My final week was in the premature baby unit and I didn't enjoy it all that much – I found the sight of all those very weak or very ill babies quite worrying after getting used to the pink-cheeked and yelling variety. I shall get used to them, I suppose, just the way I've had to get over my squeamishness in other things.

I start two weeks back in school tomorrow, then have a few days seeing the way in which the Accident and Emergency department works, then on to Male Medical followed by Home for Christmas!

It's really cold here now; we are all travelling between wards and canteen in our winter cloaks. They look very dashing and glam but in reality are draughty – all those folds for the wind to creep up! Our rooms are freezing, too; half the time the storage heaters are storing when you want them to be giving, and they never take account of when you're doing night work, either.

Is there anything special I can bring you home for Christmas? Anything special and cheap, *I should say!*

Love, Emma xxx

Southpark General
16th November

Dear Avril,
I think I'll take up gambling. I'm certainly not lucky in love and they always say it's one or the other, don't they?

It's been over two weeks since the Hallowe'en dance and I really thought I had it made with Luke. He seemed so keen – fantastic goodnight kiss, meaningful looks, everything. *Since then, not a word. I mean, what's wrong with me?*

Makes me mad, really. Here I am, a supposedly modern, liberated girl, yet I can't bring myself to ring him. I keep trying to reason with myself: why should it be me *waiting around to hear from* him, *etc.? Yet I can't make myself do it.*

I asked Bev if he'd mentioned me to Jeremy at all and she said no, though she's not seen Jeremy for more than ten minutes at a time lately because all the medics were taking their end-of-year exams.

So perhaps that's the reason, though I can't see why he couldn't spare me five minutes on the phone, just to say hello.

Trouble is, with him on my mind since I've been back in school, I've not been giving classwork and lectures my undivided attention. All I keep doing is thinking up reasons why he hasn't rung, inventing excuses for him or trying to convince myself that I'm being silly and don't like him anyway (can't make this last one stick). I emerged from the last lecture we had: Care of the Newborn in the Home, without having heard a thing. I knew this would happen if I wasn't careful.

I read the bit in your letter, about seeing Martin and Julie in the cinema, without a flicker of jealousy. You didn't mention if they were kissing the whole time but I bet they were. Thank God I haven't got to put up with all that any more. Christmas should be quite peaceful.

I hope Christmas won't be too awkward, actually. Thanks for saying that I can come with you and Paul to parties, and I expect I will, but all I hope is we don't keep falling over Martin and Julie snogging everywhere we go. Perhaps I can find a makeshift escort.

Next day

Thought *I would get pulled up. For goodness sake don't say a word to Mum, if you see her, but I've just had to go before the Director of Nurse Education. He's the chap who originally interviewed us all and he's in charge of all the different education departments. He was very nice, assured me that he wasn't exactly disciplining me, but he thought he ought to warn me that my last essays weren't really up to scratch and he wouldn't like me to fail my block (I'd have to go back and do Obstetrics again, then).*

So I'm really going to concentrate like mad from now on. That's the trouble with nursing; you just can't be less than one-hundred-per-cent efficient or they are on you like a ton of bricks. I'm going to try not to think of Whatshisname at all – oops, there goes another white-coated figure and I went all funny.

Some of us went out with the district midwives yesterday. There are practically no babies born at home now (except accidentally) but lots of mums are discharged after forty-eight hours so there's still a need for home-visiting midwives. We went to visit a first-time mum; she showed us upstairs and proudly said to me to prepare myself for 'the most beautiful baby in the world'.

I looked into the cot then looked back at her to see if she was joking – she wasn't! She picked up this fat, bald baby with the roundest face and hugest cheeks you've ever seen. He was just like a hamster!

'Isn't he lovely? Isn't he a pet?' she kept saying, and I had to lie through my teeth and say that yes, he was. Honestly, I can't understand what it is that makes each mum think her baby beautiful, really I can't.

This mum was worse than most; she talked about the baby non-stop, he was the complete centre of her world. The room was all over bunnies: bunny wallpaper, bunny cot transfers, bunny mobile and bunny lampshade. Like pets' corner.

I'm going to write up some of my notes now and make them into such a wonderfully intelligent essay that the Director of Nurse Education will be amazed and speechless.

Write soon,

Love, Emma xxx

Southpark General
23rd November

Dear Granny,
I know Mum said you didn't mind that I never had time to write to you – you read my letters to them anyway – but my first year is almost up and I can't come home knowing that I've not written once to my Gran!

This last eleven months has really zoomed. Next month we should all get our belts to signify that we've gone through a whole year's training and to distinguish us from the new student nurses starting in January. Funny to think that they're actually going to be in awe of us (or they jolly well should be).

There is a special little ceremony for the belts, the older student nurses say. We all go individually to the Director of Nurse Education and he shakes us by the hand and congratulates us, then hands the belt over. The rest of the day you keep fiddling with it and admiring your reflection whilst wearing it!

The other girls in my intake are already talking about what they want to specialize in when they finish training, but I honestly can't say. Every ward I go to I find more interesting than the one before, so I expect I'll just leave those sort of decisions until the end.

I'm sick to death of canteen meals and sardines on toast so I'm really looking forward to being at home for Christmas and having Mum make a fuss of me. I know you'll be coming to stay as usual so I'll see you soon.

Lots of love, Emma xxx

26th November
I turned in a good final essay for my block – got congratulated on it by my tutor, in fact, so I know I'll pass all right and won't have to take Obstetrics again.

Been giving myself a good talking-to about Luke. It annoys me that I can come this far: leave home, make a new career and life for myself, yet still find myself at the awful stage of hanging around waiting for someone to get in touch. The more I think about it, the more determined I feel. Why shouldn't I ring him, just for a chat? We are friends, after all. I'm not chasing him, just being casually friendly. . .

I've just looked in my purse and I've got loads of ten-pence pieces so I'm going to do it now – Right Now – before I can lose my nerve. At least I'll know where I stand.

Later
Wish I hadn't. I rang their flat and a *girl* answered. I was tempted to hang up there and then but I bravely carried on and said in what I hoped was a breezy, uncaring voice: 'Luke, please!'

'Who is it?' she said.

'Emma.'

'Emma?' in suspicious voice.

'That's right.'

Felt positively sick by the time Luke came on. Have decided *not* to be liberated from now on; *they* can do all the phoning.

He didn't seem to mind that I'd phoned, though, sounded quite pleased to hear from me. He said he'd been meaning to ring but I must 'know how it was'.

I said of course I did and I was just ringing for a chat. Following *that* I realized I didn't have anything to chat about. All I really wanted to know was – who was the girl who'd answered the phone? I had this awful feeling that she might still be there, nibbling the ear that the receiver wasn't pressed to.

Came off the phone with no date or anything, and feeling that I'd been very pushy. Went straight to see Bev who laughed like anything and said that it was just Jeremy's sister round there like she always was.

'But why's she always there?'

'She's got a flat round the corner that's crammed with people. She goes to Jeremy's to get away from them all.'

'What's she like?'

'Quite nice.'

'To look at, I mean.'

'Back of a bus,' Bev said cheerfully. 'A double-decker.'

'But does she fancy Luke?' I persisted. After all, Luke might like buses.

'I don't think so,' Bev said.

I'm not convinced. Jeremy's nice looking so I

don't see how his sister can be that bad. She's probably like Miss World only Bev doesn't like to say so.

28th November

I've been in Accident and Emergency for two days. Jon was in yesterday (with someone, not as a patient) and was waiting for me when I came off duty tonight.

'Turned up like a bad penny – or bad copper, should I say – ha ha!' he said, and he asked if I'd like to 'partake of a cuppa' with him before he went on duty.

I said yes, more for something to do than anything else, then could have kicked myself because when we got outside, Luke was standing in the ambulance bay as if he was waiting for someone.

Don't know if he was waiting for me or not, because he waved and began to walk over, then seemed to see Jon for the first time. When he got level with us he just said 'Hi!' and carried on walking into Casualty.

I'm so *mad*. Even if he wasn't waiting for me at least we could have talked a bit and maybe I could have fluttered my eyelashes at him or something. As it was I spent the entire half-hour with Jon thinking about Luke and cursing my luck.

Perhaps he thinks I'm already going out with someone. I can hardly ring him again and say that I'm not, can I?

Chapter ten

Southpark General
Sunday 6th December

Dear Mum and Dad,
Bad news first. I won't be home for Christmas.
Feel as awful about it as you do but I couldn't really get out of it. I'm on Mackay Ward now, which is a Male Medical, and two of the second-year student nurses were involved in a car accident at the weekend. It's not too serious (though one has a broken leg) but it leaves the ward permanently short over Christmas. They can't get agency nurses to work then so Sister asked if I'd like to volunteer, especially as I'm not married or anything.
So here I'll be, stuck in the hospital and on duty Christmas Day. I hope they'll let me out for New Year, though – I'll let you know as soon as I can. It might be short notice.
I expect it'll be quite jolly here. I wonder if all that going through the wards with lanterns singing Christmas carols is real or just cooked up for the films? I'll let you know!
Mackay Ward is in the new part of the hospital. Very modern, four-bedded wards, each bed has its own washbasin and there's a loo, shower and bath between four (better facilities than in the nurses'

home). Outside in the corridor there's the nursing station with Sister's office, kitchen, sluice room, etc. to cater for thirty patients.

Sister Armitage is young and terrifically glam. She's got a very pale, creamy skin and ginger hair and word has it that when she *takes blood pressures they all go up a few points! She's very nice, too, has given me lots of help and encouragement and always takes time to explain what she's doing and why. Some of the other old crows – like Sister Brunel – just expect you to know things by mind transference. The tutors from nursing school all love her, because she doesn't mind them coming in and working with us students. But some (Sister Brunel again) treat the tutors as interfering nuisances and just give them boring old routine things to do and nasty patients to work on.*

So it won't be too bad here at Christmas. I don't know what social delights there are in store but I did hear that the doctors put on a pantomime.

Don't worry about sending presents here (if you were). I'll have them when I come home – and still in a pillowcase, please.

I'll write again as soon as I know when I can get home.

Love, Emma xxx

Southpark General
15th December

Dear Avril,
You don't have to worry about carting me around to all the Christmas parties because I'm not going to be home. I'm so *valuable to the hospital, you see, that they really don't think they can manage without me.*

Actually, they are terrifically short-staffed and as I'm on such a nice ward I volunteered to work over. Merits at least a halo in that great ward up in the sky, don't you think?

I've been on Nights for the past ten days so I haven't seen anything of Luke. (You guessed it, I'm using being on Nights as an excuse as to why he hasn't contacted me.) He was waiting outside Casualty a couple of weeks ago but I don't know if it was to see me or not, because I happened to come out of there with Jon. Damn and blast! I still *don't know if he's interested in me.*

It's getting very jolly and Christmassy here already. The patients that are well enough are getting ready to go home and the longer term ones are digging themselves in. Those that are up and about are recalling Wartime-Christmasses-They-Have-Known (they are mostly getting on a bit) and one of them, who's a greengrocer, had a huge pile of mistletoe brought in yesterday.

He had a wreath brought in too, but no one seemed to want that *over their bed, so we've put it on the sluice room door. The mistletoe has been distributed round. Last night we found that someone had put a sprig of it into each thermometer container, above the beds, so they all wanted a kiss last night when we did temperature rounds! Had to decline because of the risk of cross-infection.*

17th December

Started back on Days today. On my last duty on Nights (was it yesterday or the day before? I've got jet-lag) I went into the canteen and Luke was there. He waved at me to come over to him, seemed pleased to see me, and asked me if I was off duty. I said I was just going on, but he didn't say why he'd asked (wanted to whisk me off somewhere exotic, perhaps?). The thing was, I'd just bought this huge meat-and-two-veg type meal to see me through the night, but just because he was sitting there looking at me I found I couldn't eat a thing. He only has to be close and I feel all churned up and sort of lumpy inside. Because I couldn't swallow I had to push the meal away and say it was awful, though really it was only fairly awful (which means delicious by hospital standards) and so, two hours later, I was absolutely starving. Through the quiet of the sleeping ward came the sound of my stomach, loudly protesting at being denied nourishment.

Haven't yet found out if he's on duty at Christmas. Hope *so.*

Found a great jumbled box of Christmas decorations on top of a cupboard today so passed it to two patients who sorted it out all over the dining table this morning. Loads of old paper chains, bells, balls and even an imitation tree, circa 1924 I should think. I got some foil from the kitchens and got the rest of the patients sitting up cutting out stars, and then this afternoon everything went up. Looks like Aladdin's cave in some of the side wards, especially as one chap has plastered his window with cottonwool balls from medical supplies. Don't know what the doctors are going to say.

The loveliest thing happened just before I went off duty. Mr French, a lovely old boy who's been in with pneumonia, was much better and was due to go home. It was only back to an old people's home so he was stalling a bit, but they do try and discharge as many patients as possible before Christmas so I knew there was no hope of him staying on. Anyway, he'd been speaking to the medical social worker about his family, all thought to have died long ago, and without saying anything to anyone she'd contacted the Salvation Army. Who should turn up today but his daughter*; she'd been evacuated during the war and had been told that her father had died in an air raid!*

The daughter came in with the social worker and was hidden in the kitchen while we went to try to prepare Mr French. I helped wash him, put his best pyjamas on him (and borrowed a posh silk dressing gown from one of the other patients). He looked lovely; he's got a mass of silver hair and all his own teeth (so he never tires of telling us). And there he was, sitting up in bed confused and disbelieving, when we brought her in.

It was the loveliest, most moving thing I'd ever seen. We all *cried, from Sister downwards, and even Doctor Blake had tears in his eyes. I keep crying whenever I think of it, which has been most of the evening.*

He is going home with his daughter and will live with her and her husband from now on. There are even grandchildren that he's never seen. I must stop writing about it because I'm sniffing all over the place and I can't afford any more tissues until the end of the month.

Hope you have a lovely Christmas; give everyone a kiss for me (leave out Martin, if you like). See you when I get there,

Love, Emma xxx

Diary

21st December
Got my belt today! I have now, officially, completed one year's training as a nurse. It was quite moving; we were all summoned individually to the Director's office, giving a little talk, then congratulated and shaken by the hand. Really thrilled with my belt. Can't wait to get back in January and lord it over the new students.

Bev got hers yesterday. She came out of the office with tears in her eyes, saying she was going to be the best, most considerate and caring nurse the hospital had ever trained. When I saw her an hour later she was killing herself laughing and said she'd just got into trouble with Sister for handing out the bedpans with tinsel on them!

The doctors' pantomime is being rehearsed, so Bev tells me. No one's supposed to know anything about it but apparently they 'surprise' the staff every year. It's usually *Cinderella*, with the prettiest lady doctor playing Cinders and nearly all the student doctors dressed up as ugly sisters. That's for Boxing Day. On Christmas Day the surgeons come round the wards to carve the turkeys and there's Father Christmas on the children's wards and a magician and all sorts of things. Don't know how we are supposed to nurse with all this going on.

24th December

I'm as tired as anything but know I shall never be able to sleep. There's a lot I want to get down and I'm so happy that the pen is practically skipping along the page by itself.

This evening has been quite magical. I went off duty at six but they needed a few more voices for carol singing, so I stayed. At seven o'clock we all gathered in the front hall and one of the registrars took us through the carols and gave us our song sheets, and off we went. *With* lighted lanterns.

They turned out the lights on the wards as

we approached and in we went to each one, singing 'like angels' one patient was heard to remark. The patients were completely spellbound; it was so moving that I couldn't sing for ages because of the lump in my throat, so just had to keep opening and closing my mouth at the right times.

We went through the whole building – wards, anyway, not operating theatres – and finished up in the main hall again. By this time I'd stopped being overawed and felt that I wanted to go on singing for the rest of the night.

We dispersed reluctantly and I went up the stairs to Mackay Ward to collect my bag and stuff. As I went into the locker room someone sprang out from the shadows – Luke! I was so startled (and thrilled to bits) that I was all speechless for a minute.

'Sorry if I startled you,' he said. 'I've been looking for you everywhere.'

'I've been doing the rounds, carol singing.'

'So I heard. I knew you'd come up here sooner or later.' He suddenly noticed my belt and grinned. 'Belt looks good – congratulations.'

'Thanks,' I said, looking up into those eyes again and feeling a bit wobbly.

'You can congratulate me, as well. I just heard that I'd passed my end-of-year exams – with credit, too.'

'Really? That's fantastic!' I was terribly

pleased for him – and pleased that he'd come to tell me, too. It was a strange feeling; I hardly knew him, yet right then I felt closer to him than anyone else in the world.

'How about congratulating me properly?'

'Here?' I said, looking round at the starkness of the locker room.

'Well, I can't wait much longer. Besides. . . ' and he pointed up to a bunch of mistletoe that I'd had the foresight to put up the week before.

After that it was easy! We kissed several times, and then we paused and looked at each other admiringly.

'I've been wanting to do that again ever since Hallowe'en,' he said.

'Why didn't you, then?'

'I was busy – taking exams, wondering if I ought to get involved with anyone, thinking about things – you know how it is.'

'What have you decided?'

'Nothing much. Only that I want to be with you; want to see more of you.'

We kissed again, several more times, and then the whole blissful scene was spoilt by one of the night staff coming in. Thank goodness I was off duty. We went back to his flat then, and talked some more, and now it's midnight and he's just delivered me back to the nurses' home.

I'm seeing him when I come off duty

Mum and Dad
Just a line. I will be home New
Year's Eve and please would
it be all right if I brought a
friend who has nowhere to go?!
job,
mum! because its male not female ... smashing, though!
names Luke and
midday
three days; is
I've had a
Christmas, but
missed you all. Save me
turkey.
Love,
Emma
xxx

tomorrow, and Boxing Day, and then there's all of next year to look forward to.

Bev's found a flat that she wants me to share with her, so I expect I'll move out of this room and leave a space for one of the new intake of students. It should be fun.

I'm yawning about every five words on average, but whenever I think about Luke a big Cheshire-cat grin keeps appearing on my face. I feel that I could stay awake all night, just thinking about him. Think I must be on what I've heard people call 'an emotional high'. Feels great, whatever it is.

Southpark General
26th December

Dear Mum and Dad,
Just a line. I will be home New Year's Eve – and please would it be all right if I brought a friend who has nowhere to go?!

It'll be a spare room job, Mum, because it's male not female. He's smashing, though. His name's Luke and you'll love him.

We should arrive midday and can stop three days; is that all right? I've had a wonderful Christmas, but have missed you all. Save me some cold turkey.

Love, Emma xxx